Growing Up In Kinmundy Junction

by
Kenneth Lee McGee

For Mom

This book is dedicated to the memory of my friend, Kevin Ambuehl, who was taken much too soon.

Gone... Never forgotten

Prologue

A short trip down a dusty gravel farm road brought everyone to Martin Cemetery. The wind blew gently through the large maple trees that surrounded the old hilltop cemetery. The sun shone brightly as the frail old preacher leaned on his cane to say a few final words. After Charlie was laid to rest, Robert and TyAnn walked over to see the headstone of Grandma and Grandpa Tomanek.

Robert told his sister, "I want to take a drive into town."

"Would you like some company?" TyAnn asked.

"Would you mind going with me?"

"Not at all. I haven't been to town for quite a while. I want to see the old place."

They returned to their families. Robert put an arm around his wife's waist and said, "TyAnn and I are going to take a quick run into town, Kerry. We will meet you at the church in a little while."

Kerry instinctively knew that he wanted to have some time alone with TyAnn.

"I'll ride with Kevin and help take care of our new grandson."

"Do you want me to drive you into town, Dad?" Kevin asked.

"You don't need to. TyAnn is going with me. I'll let her drive. You stay with Brandy and Ty Robert. It looks like they need you."

"Do you have your phone with you?"

"I've got it, or else your mother has it. We won't be gone too long. Start eating without us," Robert instructed Kevin.

"Oh, we will, don't worry about that," Kevin replied with a grin.

Robert looked at his son. Perhaps it was because they were at a cemetery, or maybe because he was simply feeling nostalgic, but he remembered his old friend, Kevin Ambuehl. He was the reason he named his son Kevin. He thought about the day of his funeral and recalled the cemetery outside of LaGrove where he lay. He remembered visiting the gravesite a few years ago and thought he should return soon.

Robert and TyAnn got in his car and drove away from the cemetery and headed toward Kinmundy Junction. First they drove past their grandparents' old farm. They parked the car and got out. They paused for a few minutes as they looked around. Although some of the out-buildings had been gone for years, the house, barn, machine shed and corn crib were still there. The pond and the fruit orchards survived as well. The house had a fresh coat of white paint and a new roof.

"Looks like David has been busy," Robert told TyAnn as he pointed toward the house.

"It helps to have two sons in the construction business. I'm sure Robbie and John did the work."

TyAnn noticed the pretty flowers in the front yard.

"Look at the flowers, Robert. They are just like Grandma would want!"

They spent the few minutes it took to get across the river and into town quietly lost in their own thoughts and memories. They took a back street to the old downtown area. The town had slowly changed over the years. There were some new buildings downtown, but only one grocery store now.

Robert told TyAnn, "I bet you can't put your groceries on a ledger anymore."

TyAnn looked at him and remembered. "I wonder if they still sell baseball cards?"

They headed to the cemetery to visit Mom and Dad's resting place. Someone had put out fresh flowers. *Probably Isabella,* TyAnn thought, knowing her daughter so well.

They headed back downtown, crossed the Illinois Central tracks and angled to the right. The road led to the high school. They parked in the lot and got out. The old high school building, where they spent so much time, and the gym, where Robert starred on the basketball team, had been gone for years. The big new gym, built two years after Robert graduated, even looked old now.

Robert tried to remember. "How long have I been the head coach at SIU?" he asked TyAnn.

"Thirty-four years. Almost as long as I have been teaching in the theater department," TyAnn replied.

Robert gazed at the spot where the old gym used to stand. He closed his eyes and remembered the sound of sneakers on the wooden court, the crowds cheering and he could even remember the shrill sound of the scoreboard horn. He chuckled and said, "I remember when you were the Hornets' team manager. You were so young and little."

"I did a good job, though."

"Yes, you did!"

"Let's go by the house," TyAnn whispered.

Robert started to get in the car, but she stopped him.

"Let's walk, lazy bones. It will be good for you."

Chapter One

TyAnn Allyson Benjamin let the wooden screen door slam behind her as she hurried outside. She jumped down the two porch steps and came running down the sidewalk in front of the house after her older brother and hollered, "Wait for me, Bubby!" Her brown eyes glistened as she scrambled toward the seven-year-old brother she idolized.

Big brother Robert Lee Benjamin stopped and turned around. He set his Zorro lunchbox on the ground. "TyAnn, you need to stay home," he told her when she caught up to him.

"Bubby, I want to go with you!"

"I have to go to school. You need to stay home and help Mommy."

"Will you be gone all day? Can't you come home for lunch?"

Robert dried the tears running down her cheek. "If it'll make you happy, I'll tell Mrs. Heaton that I have to come home for lunch. You can see the school from the backyard, and I will wave to you when I get there, okay?"

"Promise?" TyAnn's lip quivered. "You won't forget, will you?"

"Yes, Tanny, I promise."

TyAnn scurried to the backyard to watch for her wave from her big brother. She knew the exact spot where she needed to stand to see the front steps on the east side of the school through the large maple trees. When Robert got to the front steps, he turned, and waved as hard as he could to make sure TyAnn could see him. In the backyard TyAnn waved her short little arms at her only brother and best friend.

She went back in the house and once again asked, "Mommy, when will I be big enough to go to school with Bubby."

Emma Tomanek Benjamin very patiently answered the question for the thousandth time. "Next year you will start kindergarten, and go to school for part of the day."

TyAnn wondered how long it would be until next year. She ambled to the bedroom and picked up her old rag doll she had named "Doll Kitty." Doll Kitty had been her constant companion for over three and a half years. Mom had lovingly laundered and repaired Doll Kitty countless times over the years for TyAnn. In the meantime, she would play with her puppy. TyAnn had been allowed to name her puppy and chose the name Charger. She was a female black lab with a white streak on her chest.

TyAnn told Mom, "I'm going outside to play in the sandbox."

"Okay, sweetie. Try not to get too much sand in your hair, like yesterday."

"I'll try, Mommy," TyAnn answered as she touched her short brown hair trying to feel if there was any sand still there from yesterday. "Come on, Charger! Let's go outside and play," she called to her six-month-old puppy. Charger barked once and furiously wagged her tail.

TyAnn entertained herself until Robert came home for lunch. Robert dashed in the front door, "Hi, Mom. I came home for lunch to see Tanny. Where is she?"

"She's in the backyard with Charger."

Robert sat his lunchbox on the table and bolted out the back door. He saw TyAnn in the sandbox. She was talking to Charger while on her knees filling a small metal pail with sand.

"Tanny!" he called, "I'm home."

She jumped up and ran to see him. She threw her arms around him as he knelt down and gave her a hug. "Bubby! Where have you been? I thought you were never coming home."

"I wasn't gone that long," he teased.

"Lunch is ready!" Mom called from the back porch.

Robert and TyAnn rushed inside and sat on the red-padded metal chairs at the chrome-plated, white-topped, rectangular kitchen table. Mom had made a peanut butter and jelly sandwich for TyAnn. Robert opened his lunch box, pulled out his sandwich and thermos. They quickly ate their sandwiches, drank their whole milk and shared Robert's apple.

"May we be excused? We want to go play ball."

"Go ahead, but be careful not to hurt your sister, Robert."

James Lee Benjamin, their father, had built a seven-foot-high basketball hoop for them. With a smaller than normal size ball, Robert could shoot and make baskets easily. TyAnn struggled mightily, but she managed to make a few baskets, too.

"Good shot, Tanny. You made a basket."

"I can bounce the ball like you do. Watch!" She tried to dribble the ball, but it rolled away and Charger chased after it. She used her nose to push the ball back toward TyAnn as her tail wagged.

"Thank you, Charger. That's a good girl," Robert said as he patted her head. Charger barked as if answering, "You're welcome."

"Do you want to try again, Tanny?" Robert always encouraged his little sister to keep trying.

"I'll practice later. I think Doll Kitty is hungry. I need to feed her."

After they played for a while, Robert needed to head back to school.

"I've gotta go, Tanny, but I'll be home in a few hours."

"Okay, see you later, Bubby." She held up her arms waiting for a hug. Robert hugged her, then hollered, "I'm going back to school, Mom. I'll see you later."

He waved goodbye to TyAnn as he sprinted through the yards to school. She played for an hour until she got tired. She lay down on the "swinging bed" to take a nap. She had her blanket and Doll Kitty with her, and Charger lay under the hammock guarding her. Mom looked out the kitchen window, saw TyAnn sleeping, and smiled. She loved the many advantages of living in a small quiet town.

Chapter Two

The previous U.S. Census, taken in 1950, determined the small town of Kinmundy Junction had a population of six hundred and thirty-seven people. Most of the residents knew each other by sight, at least, if they didn't remember each other's names. The town lay nestled in a hilly, wooded area nearly surrounded by the Little Smokey River. The lazily running river flowed from the north, and half a mile before it reached the town, made a right turn before curving south, then east, and finally south again. Because of the horseshoe-shaped curve of the river, the town was almost an island. State highway 377 followed the river and provided access to the town. The surrounding area consisted mostly of small family farms cleared out of the woodland hills. The town received it's name because of the two railroads that crossed south of the river. Although small in population, the tight-knit community thrived. The well-maintained downtown boasted two grocery stores, a restaurant, a drug store with an old-fashioned soda fountain and other small businesses run by local people. In the middle of the block on the east side of Main Street stood a small whitewashed wooden building with a wood-burning stove still in use right in the middle of the building. A red, white and blue barber's pole attached to the front signified the building's business. The Doudera family had been serving as local barbers for over a hundred years. Jim Benjamin would bring Robert here whenever they needed a trim. Robert would warm his hands in front of the stove on cold winter days. Because of the town's location so far away from any other town of a large size, almost everybody shopped locally and supported each other. Kinmundy Junction took pride in its downtown area, and worked hard to keep it clean and attractive to the few visitors who happened to pass through town.

Dad Benjamin worked some nights at the local Gulf service station to earn extra money for the family, and to help out the owner, Alex Dwight, a close family friend. Robert and TyAnn often accompanied him. This gave Mom a chance to relax. TyAnn would listen for the bell that sounded inside the station whenever a customer pulled up to the lone island with two gas pumps.

"Daddy, you have a customer," she would announce as she looked out the front window.

Often she and Robert would follow Dad outside as he pumped the gas, cleaned the windshield and checked the oil. TyAnn would stand with Robert and hold his hand as Dad talked to the customer.

"Dad, can I get a pop from the machine?" Robert asked his father one evening.

"I want one, too, and some peanuts, please," TyAnn asked politely.

Dad gave them the coins they needed, and Robert helped his sister get her pop.

"I want Yoo-Hoo, Bubby."

"I know that's your favorite."

He used the bottle opener on the red Coke machine and handed her the bottle of Yoo-Hoo chocolate soda. She took a couple drinks, licked her lips, then set the bottle down.

"I want some peanuts now," she said giddily.

"Hold your hands under the opening, Tanny," Robert said as he put a penny in the machine that held the redskin peanuts they both loved. TyAnn held her little hands in the right spot as the peanuts tumbled out of the machine.

"I'll share with you, Bubby!"

"Thanks, Tanny," Robert replied gratefully.

The town also took pride in it's school. The forty-year-old, two-story red brick school building housed classrooms for grades K-12. Although starting to show some signs of age, the building was still in fairly good condition. The intimate and cozy gymnasium had been built on the edge of the school property three years after the school opened. A gravel parking area separated the school and the gym. Robert and TyAnn attended all the basketball games with their father, a part-time coach. Robert dreamed of the day when he would be a player on the local team called the Hornets. TyAnn enjoyed watching the games, but the popcorn she shared with Bubby interested her more. Too small for a football program, the Hornets basketball and baseball games were big events. Folks from all around the area would pack the three rows of wooden bleachers, which lined both sides of the gym, whenever there was a game. Even the baseball games drew a crowd of

12

enthusiastic supporters. Although the basketball team won more often than they lost during the regular season, they had never advanced out of the state regional tournament. Robert dreamed of the day when he would wear a purple and gold Hornet's uniform, lead his team to the championship game and make the winning shot.

Chapter Three

Mom hummed a tune as she kept busy making supper in her small, brightly-painted yellow kitchen. She opened the door to the brand new white General Electric refrigerator and found only two eggs. She called Robert into the kitchen.

"Robert, would you and TyAnn run to the store for me, please? I need a few things to finish making supper. I need half a dozen eggs, a loaf of bread and two cans of tomato soup."

"Sure, Mom. Can I get some baseball cards, too?" Robert asked.

"Okay, you can get one pack, if you think they might be new ones," Mom told him.

Robert went to find TyAnn. "Mom wants us to go to the store for her," he called to his sister.

"I wanna go, I wanna go!" she cried.

Robert said, "We need to hurry because Mom needs this stuff right away to make supper."

As they walked to the corner hand in hand, TyAnn would giggle and jump every time she saw a crack in the old concrete sidewalk. They crossed the street and started down the big hill to the large mulberry tree, where they always stopped, to see if the berries were in season. TyAnn wanted some berries, so Robert held onto her as they climbed on a concrete block next to the sidewalk. She grabbed some berries and offered to share them with Robert.

TyAnn looked down the narrow side street to the right and saw the deserted little building that stood there. It was hardly more than a shack covered entirely in black tar paper and surrounded by weeds, trees and overgrown brush.

She squeezed Robert's hand, pointed at the shack and asked, "Does a wicked witch really live there?"

"No, why would you ask that, Tanny?"

"Timmy Crane told me that a wicked old witch lives there, who eats little girls."

"He was just trying to scare you. Nobody lives there anymore. It's an old shack that used to be part of a power plant before," Robert explained.

"What's a power plant?" TyAnn asked.

"I'm not sure 'xactly, but I think it used to make the lights

14

in town work," Robert replied.

They continued on their way to the downtown shopping area, and walked up the gently sloping hill to the railroad station. TyAnn held tightly to Bubby's hand as they crossed the two sets of Illinois Central railroad tracks. She looked over her shoulder at the gray station building and wondered what was inside.

Robert sternly told her, "Mom doesn't want you to come here by yourself and cross the tracks alone. It's too dangerous."

She nodded her head, "I won't, Bubby, I promise. Not 'til I get big like you!"

They turned right on Main Street and entered the downtown area. Although only three blocks long, the business district seemed so big to TyAnn. She looked up at the big buildings in awe. They stepped into the grocery store operated by Jessie Gregory. Robert said hello to the lady behind the counter. TyAnn waved to her after she called her by name. Robert took a shopping basket and looked for the soup. He was old enough to read the labels, and found the tomato soup quickly. He showed it to TyAnn.

"Can you tell me what the letters are, Tanny?"

She looked at the letters and, with pride, correctly named each one. Robert found the bread and eggs, and they took their basket to the front counter. He picked up a pack of baseball cards and told the lady at the counter, "Mom said I could have one pack today!"

"These just came in yesterday. I hope you get some new players."

The lady placed their groceries in two bags for them to carry home. TyAnn told the lady goodbye, and outside the store she asked Bubby. "Does it cost money to buy food at the store?"

"I think it does," he answered. "We'll ask Mom when we get home."

"Yes, it costs money to buy groceries!" Mom later replied with a chuckle and a smile.

"Then how come we never take any money with us?" Robert asked, with a serious look on his face.

Mom explained, "Mrs. Gregory knows you are the Benjamin kids, and writes how much the groceries cost on our ledger. Once a month your father pays the bill. That way I can send you to the store without any money."

15

TyAnn asked, "What's a ledger, Mommy?"

Robert answered, "That must be the piece of paper I saw her writing on, right, Mom?"

"That's right, Robert, and every month Mrs. Gregory starts a new ledger."

Robert asked, "How much do baseball cards cost?"

"A nickel," Mom replied.

Robert walked to the bedroom he shared with TyAnn and brought back a shiny new nickel he had earned by doing small chores. He gave it to Mom, "This is to help pay the bill, Mom!"

Mom smiled at him and gave him a big hug.

Chapter Four

Mom and Dad had been shopping at Floyd's Furniture Store in Millstown for bunk beds for the kids.

"Jim, we can't afford to pay this much, but the kids need new beds. Robert has outgrown his and so will TyAnn before we know it," Emma said as she sighed.

They left the store and headed back home.

"I have an idea," Jim said as he tapped the steering wheel with his hand.

"What?" Mom wondered aloud.

"I think with a little help from your father, I could build a set of bunk beds. That way all it would cost would be the material."

The two men talked about it that Sunday afternoon. Grandpa agreed to help, since he had built all the beds for the farmhouse. Grandpa bought the necessary materials during the week and even purchased two new mattresses. On Saturday, they started building the new beds.

Dad explained to the kids, "The beds will be stacked on top of each other to allow more room to play."

Robert helped as much as he could. He would hold one end of the tape measure as Dad used a pencil to make his marks. TyAnn helped, too. She would hold the hammer for Grandpa and hand it to him when he needed it. Robert and TyAnn shared a room in the small house. Mom and Dad used the only other bedroom.

When Dad and Grandpa finally had the new beds finished, Robert immediately claimed the top bed for himself. He climbed up the ladder at the end of the bed and began to bounce. TyAnn climbed on the bottom bed and started bouncing too. She stopped as the bed began to move.

"Bubby, stop bouncing like that. You might break the bed and crash on top of me."

"I won't break the bed, Tanny. Dad and Grandpa built it real good and strong!"

Mom called, "Supper is ready! Come and eat before it gets cold."

TyAnn was thrilled to have a bed as big as Robert's to call her own.

An old fashioned bathtub, placed under the window, took up one wall of the tight bathroom located next to the two bedrooms. Robert and TyAnn didn't seem to mind not having a shower, since they had never seen one before. They enjoyed playing in the tub with their toy boats. Dad and Mom, however, were saving money for the day they could build an addition to the house.

"If we can ever afford to add on to this place, I would love to have a larger bathroom," Emma reminded Jim.

"So would I. I stopped in at Bowman's Hardware. I saw a bathtub with a shower."

"I would love to have a shower. I've never lived anywhere that had a shower in the bathroom."

"There was one in that motel we stayed at on our honeymoon," he reminded her.

Emma blushed at the memory.

The living room and dining area were on the west side of the almost square shaped house. Though small, the kitchen had enough room for the table where they ate most of their meals. In back of the kitchen was a utility room with a washer and dryer and a big freezer for food. Mom appreciated the many windows in the utility room which allowed for plenty of natural light, and also allowed her to watch the kids as they played in the backyard. Tacked onto the back of the utility room was an old porch that Dad always threatened to tear down. TyAnn didn't want Daddy to tear down the porch because she played there with Bubby during the cold winter months. Although unheated, it was still warmer than outside.

Chapter Five

Jim Benjamin had been teaching in Bedford Mills, a town over two hours away, for the last two years. This meant he could only be home weekends. During the week he would stay with his older brother, John Benjamin, and his wife Doris, who also taught at Bedford Mills High School. This year Jim returned to the high school in Kinmundy Junction to once again teach math. Mom was very grateful to have him home all the time now, even if he didn't make as much money. The kids were thrilled to have Daddy back too.

TyAnn had enjoyed being in kindergarten the previous year and now started first grade. She was so proud to be in school all day long. She walked to school everyday with Robert, now a fourth grader, and he looked after her. One day two older boys started picking on her during recess and she started crying. Robert sprinted over in a flash, and knocked the two older kids to the ground. They got up and tried to take a punch at him, but he knocked them down again.

"Don't you ever hurt her again, or I will beat you up!" Robert shouted. He picked TyAnn up. "Are you okay, Tanny? Did they hurt you?"

"I'm all right now. Why did they do that? They made fun of me and called me a bad name."

"They are bullies, but I don't think they will ever bother you again."

She stopped crying and smiled at her Bubby.

In class one day TyAnn's teacher, Mrs. Pierce, called her Annie, and in her most serious voice, TyAnn told her teacher, "Only my Bubby can call me that or Tanny."

"I'm sorry, TyAnn. I didn't realize how you felt, and I promise I will call you TyAnn from now on."

"You can call me Ty if you want, Mrs. Pierce. I don't mind if old people call me Ty."

Mrs. Pierce, now in her mid-sixties and close to retirement, saw TyAnn's mom later that day. Mrs. Pierce taught Emma Tomanek years before at a one room schoolhouse out in the country called Green Ridge School.

19

"Hello, Emma, how are you?"

"I'm doing fine, Mrs. Pierce. How is your class this year?"

"I have a great group of kids. They are all so well behaved. It's strange, though, there are only five girls in the whole class. I've never had that before. Oh, by the way, I made the mistake of calling TyAnn 'Annie' in class today. She informed me, most seriously, that I should not call her that."

Mom smiled and explained, "The kids have called each other Tanny and Bubby since they learned to talk, and TyAnn doesn't like anyone else to call her anything other than TyAnn or Ty. She won't even let me or Jim call her Tanny."

"She informed me that I could call her Ty." Mrs. Pierce chuckled as she recalled what TyAnn told her earlier. "She informed me that 'old people' could call her that."

"Oh, Mrs. Pierce, I'm so sorry."

"No need to be. To her I must seem older than dirt. She is such a precious child. She's very smart and totally a tomboy."

Mom sighed and said, "I know. She doesn't have many girls on our street to play with. Sometimes she plays with Linda Bowden, but they always end up fighting."

Mrs. Pierce didn't call TyAnn by her nickname anymore.

One day TyAnn casually mentioned to Mom, "Can I have a baby sister to play with?"

Mom looked at her and said, "I'm sorry, Ty, but your father and I won't ever have any more babies. I know you wish you had a sister to play with."

TyAnn looked at Mom and told her, "Don't be sad, Mommy, Bubby and I have each other to play with. I guess I don't mind if I never have a little sister."

Mom was grateful that the kids were so close and such good friends. There weren't any kids TyAnn's age in the neighborhood. The next door neighbors were both older couples whose children were grown and even had kids of their own.

Chapter Six

Although TyAnn loved going to school, she looked forward to Sunday afternoons. The family went to church in the morning, then traveled across the river, and out to the farm where Grandma and Grandpa Tomanek lived. Most of the time all the aunts and uncles were there with their families. Robert and TyAnn played outside with their cousins, while the grownups sat in the house and talked. Grandma could always be found in the kitchen making pies and other good food to eat. Sometimes Grandma would let TyAnn climb on a chair to help.

One Sunday as they were on the way to the farm TyAnn asked Mom, "Why don't we ever go to see my other grandma and grandpa anymore?"

Mom told her, "Both of your other grandparents are gone now, honey."

TyAnn asked, "Where did they go?"

Robert explained, "They are both dead because they had the cancer disease."

TyAnn didn't understand. When they got to the farm, Dad held her on his lap and tried to explain to her what happened to his parents. TyAnn cried because her dad seemed sad. "I don't want you or Mommy to ever get the cancer disease."

Dad hugged her and kissed her cheek. "Don't cry, baby. We aren't sick."

TyAnn liked to answer the phone at Grandma's house and didn't understand when Grandma told her, "That's not our ring."

"It's really ringing, Grandma. I can hear it."

Grandma tried to explain to TyAnn that they shared the phone with other people, and they only answered the phone when it rang three short times. TyAnn would forget, and one day she answered the phone after the wrong ring.

"Hello, this is my Grandma's house," she said to the person on the other end.

The voice on the other end asked, "Is this Joe Polanka's?"

"This is Grandma and Grandpa's house!" TyAnn told the voice again.

Mom heard TyAnn talking on the phone and asked, "Who

21

are you talking to, honey?"

"Some man wants to talk to Joe P'lonka," she told Mom.

"Let me talk to him, honey."

"Okay. I'm sorry if I did something wrong, Mommy."

"It's okay, baby. Why don't you see if Grandma needs some help in the kitchen?"

TyAnn walked to the kitchen and Mom took the phone. "I'm sorry. My little girl answered the phone by mistake," Mom explained to Mr. Salter, who lived a couple of miles away.

"That's all right, Mrs. Benjamin. I do that myself sometimes. How is everyone at the farm doing?"

"Mom and Dad are both doing fine."

Mom talked to Mr. Salter for a moment before she hung up to let him make his call again.

TyAnn liked to play sports with all the boys. They would let her play football and would carefully toss the ball to her. More often than not, she would catch it and take off running in whatever direction she wanted. She would be so serious as she raced around the barnyard with the ball. She learned how to swing a bat and how to watch the ball in order to hit it.

One Sunday afternoon, as they were taking a break from the softball game, TyAnn needed a drink of water. Robert lowered the bucket into the well in the front yard. He let the bucket sink to the bottom where the water would be the coolest. He struggled to pull it back up, but managed to get it to the top without spilling too much. He used the metal dipper and let TyAnn have the first drink. After they had quenched their thirst, she asked Robert, "Why aren't there any other girl cousins besides me?"

"No one else wanted to have girl babies because they are not as much fun to play with, and when they grow up they can't work on the farm."

"Don't you think I'm fun to play with?" TyAnn asked him as she started to get upset. She put her hands on her hips, as she had seen Mom do, and glared at Robert.

Robert stopped teasing and said, "I'm just kidding. You are fun to play with, and we will keep you in the family."

They ran back toward the barnyard to resume playing ball. TyAnn waved at Grandma, who was working on one of her flower beds, and didn't watch where she was going. She tripped on the narrow sidewalk, fell and scraped her knee. It started to bleed right away. She looked at her bloody knee and started crying.

"Bubby! Go get Mommy! I fell down and hurt my knee."

Robert heard her and immediately raced back to her. "Tanny, you scraped your knee."

"It hurts, Bubby. Go get Mommy!" she wailed as she sat in the grass.

He picked her up and held her in his arms as he carried her to the back of Grandma's house. He sat her down on the wooden porch steps and bolted inside to find Mom. Grandma came over to check on TyAnn.

"Mom, come quick!" he cried out. "Tanny fell down, and she's bleeding."

He hustled back to his sister, and held her hand. Mom came outside, saw the problem and knew it was not serious. She went into the bathroom and brought out a washcloth, some Mercurochrome and a Band-aid. Robert took the supplies from his mom.

"I will take care of Tanny by myself, Mom. I learned how in Cub Scouts. You can watch to see if I do it right, and maybe I can earn a badge."

"Okay. Let's see if you know how to do first-aid." Mom smiled at him and watched.

Robert cleaned her cut with the washcloth. "Tanny, this might sting a little when I put it on."

She nodded her head but didn't cry as Robert fixed her cut.

He finished and asked, "Are you all right now? Does it still hurt?"

"I'm okay now," she replied as she gave Bubby a hug.

They scurried off to play some more as Mom watched from the porch. Soon Robert and TyAnn were climbing trees, and she forgot all about her skinned knee.

Chapter Seven

Time passed and the Benjamin family still went out to the farm every Sunday to see Grandma and Grandpa Tomanek. Being the only girl, and the youngest of all the grandkids, TyAnn was spoiled by her grandparents.

TyAnn and Robert loved playing in the woods at the farm. It was more fun than playing at home in town. She played "forts" and "Cowboys and Indians" with the boys. The farm seemed so big to her and most of the land was wooded, which made it a great place to have adventures. Grandpa Tomanek had dug a pond when he first built the farm, and TyAnn and Robert loved to go fishing with him. She knew how to dig up worms for bait, and caught fish just as often as her brother. One day when they were fishing, she caught a turtle and wanted to keep it as a pet. When she got it home, Charger tried to attack the turtle. The kids also used the large pond as a swimming hole. TyAnn learned to swim at a very young age and was like a fish in the water.

There were two orchards on the hundred and fifty acre farm. West of the barn, between the barn and the pond was an apple orchard. South of the machine shed, on the side of a hill, was a pear orchard. The kids helped themselves to the apples and pears when they were in season. Grandma had a large garden area south of the house. A wire fence surrounded the entire garden. Just to the left of the garden gate was one of the out-buildings. A low building, barely six feet tall at the highest point, built of wood with four foot square openings on the back side, that Grandma always referred to as the turkey shed. TyAnn would often peek inside to see if there were any turkeys. Only once did she ever see a live turkey in the shed. The turkey saw TyAnn and began chasing her. TyAnn sprinted to the wooden gate and climbed to the top to escape.

Grandma planted every kind of vegetable imaginable. Beans, carrots, onions, potatoes and many others that Grandma would preserve and store in the cellar under the house. There were strawberries and watermelons in the garden and a grape arbor along one side of the garden. TyAnn loved to suck the juice out of the grapes. One day she had so many grapes that she got sick to her stomach. She ran in the house to tell Mom.

"Mommy, I threw up outside. My belly hurts."

"Have you been eating the grapes again? How many did you have, honey?"

"I stopped counting when I got to thirty!"

"No wonder you were sick," Grandma said. "Come and help me make some cookies, that will help you feel better."

TyAnn climbed up on a chair to help Grandma.

Later that day, TyAnn's two oldest cousins, Dwayne and Ed, returned from deer hunting. They would often go deer hunting in the woods even if it was not officially hunting season. Dwayne always liked to tease TyAnn, and he picked her up and tossed her up in the air.

TyAnn told Dwayne, "You smell funny. What have you been doing?"

Dwayne answered, "Ed and I have been hunting all day and shot a six point buck. We were in the corn crib..." At this point Dwayne realized that TyAnn was giving him a funny look and he stopped talking about the buck.

TyAnn looked very seriously at him and asked, "Did you shoot a poor helpless deer, Dwayne?" TyAnn looked about as angry as a little girl could be. Dwayne nodded his head.

"Put me down this instant! I'm telling Uncle Gus what you did when I see him," TyAnn said with all the ferocity she could muster. She fled back to Grandma, and didn't talk to Ed or Dwayne for the rest of the day.

Chapter Eight

It was July and summer vacation was halfway over. Before school started, Mom needed to have a talk with her daughter. "TyAnn, Robert is going to start sleeping on the couch in the living room for now."

"Why, Mommy?"

TyAnn didn't understand why, so Mom explained, "You are both getting older, and you need your privacy. We have saved enough money to put an addition on the house before school starts. Then you and Robert will each have your own bedroom."

"Is that why there is all that lumber in the backyard?"

"Yes, Grandpa and all your uncles and your father are going to start the new addition this weekend. You and Bubby can decide who gets which of the current bedrooms."

"It might be nice to have my own room. Can I keep the bunk beds, or will Bubby have to use them in his room?"

"Your father and I are buying a new bedroom set for us. We will leave our old bed and dresser where they are, so if you want to keep the bunk beds in your room, you can."

"If I do that, I can have friends sleep over!"

Later that day TyAnn talked to Robert about the bedrooms. "Did you know that Daddy is going to make the house bigger?"

"Yes, I've known that for several months."

"Mommy said we will each have a bedroom, but we have to choose. Which one do you want?" she asked as they walked into their parents' room.

"I thought it might be better if I move in here, Tanny. That window opens onto the front porch, and I thought that might scare you."

"I wouldn't be scared because Charger would be with me, but you can have this room. I like where I sleep now."

"You want to be able to sleep on the bunk beds," Robert teased.

Robert decided to move into his parents' old bedroom, so TyAnn stayed put.

With help from Grandpa, all the uncles and some of the older cousins, the new addition, on the west side of the house, didn't take long to finish. Robert was allowed to help, but TyAnn had to be content with watching. She made herself useful by bringing cold lemonade to the men. Uncle Charlie liked to tease TyAnn, and she always had fun with him.

Soon, Mom and Dad enjoyed their first night sleeping in their brand new bedroom. TyAnn was surprised when she found out that they had another bathroom, as well. She didn't know anyone who had two bathrooms in their house. Mom even let TyAnn take her first ever shower in the new bathroom. After a few nights, Mom noticed that TyAnn didn't sleep in the same bed all the time.

"Why are you sleeping in both beds, honey?"

"Well, sometimes Charger goes to bed first, and she likes the bottom bed. I don't want to wake her up, so I use the top bunk. If I go to bed first, Charger sleeps on the floor, or with Bubby."

For as long as Mom could remember, TyAnn had been afraid of storms. Whenever it would storm at night, she would climb in bed with her Bubby for protection. Shortly after Robert moved out of her room, there was a bad thunderstorm at night. One particularly loud clap of thunder woke TyAnn up, and she was afraid. She whispered for Bubby, forgetting he was not in the room. Robert heard the storm, and realized TyAnn was probably afraid if she was awake. He tiptoed into her room, and she called out to him.

"I don't like the thunder and lightning. It feels like the wind is going to knock the house down."

"The house is good and sturdy, Tanny. Nothing will happen to it. The storm will be over soon."

"Can I stay with you until it's over?"

"Okay, but you have to go to sleep. Come on, Charger. You can stay with us." She followed Robert into his room and soon fell back asleep with his arm around her protecting her.

In the morning Mom checked on the kids, and was surprised not to see TyAnn in bed. She looked in Robert's room and found both kids sound asleep on the bed with Charger between them. Charger looked up at Mom.

"Did you keep the kids safe last night, Charger? You understand about storms, don't you?"

Charger barked once and wagged her tail, as if she was answering the question.

Chapter Nine

The years passed slowly in the sleepy little town and in time Kinmundy Junction had grown to over nine hundred people. Outside of town, the last of the one-room schoolhouses had closed. Green Ridge School closed it's doors for the last time. At one time the countryside had been dotted with over thirty of the unique schools. Now they had all been shuttered—many of the buildings had been abandoned. Others found new life as homes, or in a couple of cases, as churches. Because all of the kids who lived outside of town would now be coming to town for school, Kinmundy Junction needed more classrooms. The old building was bursting at the seams. The school board reached a decision the previous year. They needed to build a new school, but weren't sure where to put the new building. The discussion ended when one of the local farmers decided to donate the land. He had enough acres at the edge of town for a small grade school. Construction began and a year later the new grade school was dedicated. Grades one through five would now be taught in the brand new building.

Until this year, Robert had always walked to school and back home with TyAnn everyday. She still idolized her big brother, and they were best friends. Dad taught in the high school, and Mom stayed home, except when she would substitute teach. Now, in order to start saving money for the kid's college education, Mom decided to start teaching full-time at the new school. She taught second grade. TyAnn would be in fourth grade, and Robert in seventh grade when school started again. TyAnn was disappointed that she was not in the same school building as Robert, but at least Mom was with her. She couldn't wait until she was in sixth grade and back in the old building.

Most of the time, TyAnn kept her long curly brunette hair in a ponytail. Her expressive brown eyes were full of curiosity. TyAnn didn't realize that when she was older, the boys were going to be captivated by her looks.

Now in his second year of junior high, Robert played on the basketball team and was the best player, by far. His cousins, David and Chuck Tomanek, were also on the team. The three cousins had a great year on the junior high Warriors basketball team, and they didn't lose a single game. Robert was the team's point guard, and scored the most points and had the most rebounds, as well. TyAnn watched every game, even the ones played in other towns. She liked traveling to the other small towns with her father. Mom went to most of the games, but sometimes had to stay home—a housewife's job never seemed to end. TyAnn enjoyed watching the cheerleaders and even practiced with them occasionally. She told Mom about a goal she had.

"Since there isn't a girls basketball team, I want to be a cheerleader when I'm in sixth grade."

"I think you will make an excellent cheerleader, honey. I know you would rather play basketball, but at least the cheerleaders get to go to all the games."

TyAnn and Mom walked home together everyday after school while the weather was nice. During the cold winter months, Dad picked them up, or they got a ride from one of the other teachers. TyAnn heard Mom and Dad discussing the possibility of getting a second car one evening.

"Jim, it would be so convenient if we had a second car, but we can't afford one."

"We might be able to afford an older used car. I could let you have the Chevy to use, and I could drive the older car if I need to. I wouldn't have to use it every day, just when the weather is bad. What do you think, Emma? Should I look around for a used car?"

"You can look, but it would have to be something cheap!"

Dad asked around and found a ten-year-old Ford that Mrs. Newcastle was selling. Her father had used the car until he passed away.

"Jim, you can have the car for a hundred dollars. I don't need it. Is that a fair deal?"

"I think it's very fair, Mrs. Newcastle."

Dad used the new "old" car for several years and always told Mom, "It was the best hundred dollars I ever spent!"

Chapter Ten

On September 8, 1959, a Tuesday morning, after Mom and TyAnn had been at school for an hour, the town fire siren sounded. Seconds later the school fire alarm rang throughout the building.

Mrs. Boyd got the attention of her fourth grade class and announced, "Okay, kids, this is a fire drill. We will have to march outside and stay together. Now let's get in a line and follow me. We will go out the side door and stay in the grass by the swing sets."

Their class traipsed out and eventually moved to their assigned spot. Some of the teachers gathered together to talk. TyAnn became frightened because some of the teachers seemed to be afraid of something. She noticed that her teacher, Mrs. Boyd, seemed to be keeping calm and assuring the other teachers that everything would be all right. Mom came over to tell TyAnn that the lumber yard might be on fire, and they had to go home. The lumber yard was at the edge of town, only a short distance to the north from the school.

After a few minutes Mrs. Boyd told her students, "We are going back to our classroom, but we will have to go to the high school. The buses will be here in a few minutes to take us. I need all of you to stay together and we will all ride on the same bus."

The buses came quickly, and took all the kids over to the high school for safety. On the short ride to the old school, TyAnn, and the other kids, could see the dense black smoke from the fire. When they arrived at the high school, TyAnn noticed all the students standing outside. She saw her brother, and ran over to hold his hand. Some of the other boys started to make fun of her for being afraid, but Robert silenced them with a glare.

TyAnn saw Mom as she arrived and asked, "Where is Daddy? Bubby said he wasn't here, but he wouldn't tell me where he is."

Mom told her, "He is helping the other men fight the fire, baby."

TyAnn looked at Robert, "Don't worry, Tanny! Nothing will happen to Daddy." Robert assured her that Dad would be all right. TyAnn still worried and Mom did, too.

The town had a volunteer fire department, and though they

responded quickly, the fire spread faster than they could handle. A fire truck from the closest town, LaGrove, was on the way, but the fire soon engulfed the entire lumber yard. It would end up burning to the ground.

Mr. Woods, the high school principal talked to the faculty and staff. "I have been on the phone with Mr. Frank." Paul Frank, the school district superintendent, had been one of the first firefighters to arrive at the lumber yard. "He instructed me to cancel classes for the rest of the day and send all the students home. The only students who can't go home are the Mulvaney and Metcalf kids. Their homes are too close to the lumber yard. Mrs. Heicher has agreed to take the kids home with her until it's safe for them to go home. Does anyone have any questions?"

"Will all the students fit on the buses?" Mrs. Heicher, the school secretary asked.

"Yes, I told the high school students to look after the younger kids and make sure their siblings get on the right bus. Mr. McKitrick will supervise all the students who live in town. They will ride a bus home today. I don't want any students to be walking home. If the wind changes direction, there will be smoke blowing through town."

Within an hour all the students were loaded onto the proper bus and taken home.

The fire continued smoking and smoldering until late at night. Several times new flames would flare up and have to be dowsed. A fire truck came from Millstown to relieve some of the local firefighters. Mom tried to get the kids to bed, but they wanted to wait for Dad to get home. Mom got a phone call from one of the neighbors telling her that two of the firefighters were hurt when a wall collapsed on them. The neighbor didn't know who the two men were. Mom was really worried now, but knew she had to keep it together in front of the kids. They were up until nearly midnight before Dad pulled into the driveway and came walking in the front door covered in black soot, smelling like smoke and completely exhausted. Mom hurried to him and kissed him despite his soot covered face. Dad smiled wearily at her and asked the kids.

"What are you still doing up this late on a school night?"

TyAnn said, "We were waiting to hear about the fire. Are

we going to have school tomorrow? Please tell me the school didn't burn down."

"The school is all right, and there will be school in the morning. I will tell you all about it in the morning. Now off to bed," Dad said.

Robert and TyAnn went to their rooms, got into bed. They tried to get some sleep, but they were both wide awake and listened as Mom and Dad talked.

"Oh, Jim! I was so afraid, then I heard about the men who were hurt. No one seemed to know who was hurt."

"The two men who were hurt were from LaGrove."

"Were they seriously injured?"

"I don't think so. We got them out as quick as we could. I'm pretty sure they will be all right."

"Does anyone know how the fire started?"

"I heard someone say it was from some faulty wiring."

"Let's get you out of those clothes and into the shower."

Chapter Eleven

It was the summer of 1961, and Robert would be starting high school in the fall. TyAnn would be entering sixth grade. This meant she would be back at the same school building as Robert and also their father.

At supper one evening Dad mentioned, "Ty, in a few years when you are in Algebra class you will have to call me Mr. Benjamin. I don't want the other students to think I treat you any differently."

"Okay, Daddy. Does Bubby call you Mr. Benjamin?"

"Yes, he always does, if he calls anything me at all. Lots of times he doesn't ask me any questions."

"How about David and Chuck? Do they call you Uncle Jim?" TyAnn asked as she grinned.

"No, they call me Mr. Benjamin."

"If I had Mommy for a teacher, I could never call her Mrs. Benjamin. I would call her Mommy."

Over the summer Robert grew four inches and now stood six feet tall. Mom had a difficult time trying to buy clothes for him. "Robert, if you keep growing like this, you won't have any pants to wear."

"I can't help it. I'll look kinda silly wearing these jeans."

TyAnn saw what he had on. "You look like you're ready to go wading in the creek out back of the field at the farm."

"All I need to do is take off my shoes."

Robert played basketball every day, and worked hard to become an even better player. TyAnn watched him practice, and helped him by rebounding the ball for him and passing it back to him. She had become a good player herself.

Robert told her one day, "It's too bad you're a girl because you are a better player than most of the boys your age. Maybe someday the school will have a girl's team, and you can play on it."

"I could pretend to be a boy," TyAnn said.

"Oh, yeah! And maybe Hollywood will make a movie out of it," Robert told her sarcastically.

"It could happen!" TyAnn snapped back.

"Which?" Robert asked, "The movie or girls playing basketball."

"Both," TyAnn said as Robert laughed at her. "Bubby, when is Daddy coming home?"

"Mom said he will be gone for one more week."

Dad had been working a summer job for an insurance company. Sometimes he was gone for two weeks at a time.

"How come he has to work in the summer when Mom doesn't?" TyAnn asked Robert.

"He has to work because you eat too much," Robert teased.

"I don't eat nearly as much as you." She started chasing him around the backyard. She caught him, and he fell to the ground laughing. TyAnn straddled him and tried to tickle him. Robert pretended it actually tickled for a moment. TyAnn got up and Robert said, "I'm going to catch you and tickle the back of your knees."

She squealed, and ran away, but not fast, or far, enough. Robert caught her and pinned her to the ground.

"Bubby, stop!" TyAnn cried as she laughed.

Charger galloped after both of them and stopped to lay in the grass beside her. TyAnn put her arms around Charger and told her, "Charger, you have to protect me from Bubby because he is being mean to me. He tackled me. You need to make him stop."

Charger wagged her tail as she barked at TyAnn. Charger licked her face as TyAnn hugged her. Charger was content to let TyAnn rest her head on her side. Charger kept her eyes open for anyone who might come around. Charger was very protective of the whole family, but especially TyAnn.

Chapter Twelve

In late August school started. Dad, Robert and TyAnn would often walk the block and a half together. TyAnn was happy to be back in the same building as her brother, although she missed Mom being with her. For the first time, she had to move from one classroom to another for the different subjects. This made her feel more grown-up. She would wave whenever she saw Robert or her cousins, David and Chuck. Robert would wave back, but David and Chuck would tease her. Her girlfriends thought the guys were cute. TyAnn thought they looked like dorks.

Robert couldn't wait for basketball season to begin. Coach Anderson thought they would have a good basketball team this year. With Robert playing varsity, they would have one of the better point guards in the conference, even though he was only a freshman. Basketball season finally arrived, and the first day of practice was a disappointment for Robert. Though clearly the best player on the team, Robert had to endure some petty jealousy from his senior teammates. They didn't think a freshman should be starting and tried to make Robert look bad. Coach Anderson let them continue for awhile, then blew his whistle. He brought them all over to the sidelines and sat them down. Coach proceeded to let them have an earful.

"In case you guys haven't learned this by now, let me explain it to you once again. Basketball is a team sport! Got that? A team sport. If you are unwilling to play together as a team, you are not going to be successful. If you seniors don't want to play as a team, then you will be watching from the bench. I will play the guys who play best as a team. We had a decent team last year, and this year we can do even better... but only if we play as one unit."

To prove his point he had a scrimmage between the junior varsity and the varsity. The varsity players, all seniors, played as individuals while the junior varsity played as a unit. Robert played for the junior varsity, and they won by fifteen points in a twenty minute scrimmage. Coach Anderson got his point across, and the seniors fell in line. With the combination of the experienced seniors and the more talented freshman, they had a deep team.

TyAnn tried out to be a junior high cheerleader but didn't make the squad. Miss Powell explained the reason to her, "I know you are disappointed, TyAnn. I'm sorry, but I can only keep six girls. This year we had more eighth grade girls try out than we expected. Since this is their last year in junior high, I chose them. You are athletic, and I'm sure you will make the squad next year."

"I understand, Miss Powell. Would you mind if I watch practice whenever I can? I want to be part of the team somehow."

"Of course you can, Ty. Who knows, we might need a replacement if one of the girls gets hurt."

TyAnn learned the routines quickly, but didn't get a chance to sub for any of the other girls.

TyAnn usually met Robert after basketball practice and they shot baskets. Coach Anderson saw her shooting and dribbling with Robert. "I see basketball talent still runs in the family," Coach Anderson told them.

TyAnn asked Coach, "Is there anything I can do to help during practice?"

Coach thought for a moment, then asked her, "Can you run the clock?"

TyAnn smiled and answered, "Of course I can. Daddy showed me how."

"What about making sure the players have clean towels and water?" Coach asked TyAnn thinking she would not be so excited about that.

"I'll do anything," she replied.

Coach rubbed his jaw and said, "All right. Be here after school for practice, and we'll see how you do."

She walked home with Robert and told Mom, "I have a job!"

"What do you mean you have a job? What kind of job?" Mom asked.

Robert told Mom what Coach Anderson wanted her to do. "She will run the clock during our scrimmages, and make sure the guys have towels and plenty of water. After practice, she will have to clean out the locker room, and do all the laundry and scrub the gym floor..."

TyAnn's eyes grew as big as saucers as she listened to Robert.

Robert looked at her and smiled. "I'm just kidding, Tanny. You don't really have to scrub the gym floor. You only have to sweep it!"

TyAnn knew he was still teasing her. "If that's what Coach wants, then that's what I'll do!"

Dad heard them talking and asked, "Are you sure you want to try this, honey? It sounds like a lot of responsibility for a young girl."

"Please let me try," TyAnn pleaded.

Dad called Coach Anderson, "Jim, I will keep an close eye on TyAnn, and if I think the 'job' is too much for her, I will let you know. Steve Winkler is the regular team manager, and he will have most of the responsibilities. TyAnn seems to love basketball almost as much as Robert. I think this will be a good experience for her."

"Okay, I will let her try it for a while," Dad informed Coach Anderson.

Soon it was time for the first game of the season. This year their first game was against a much bigger school, North Clay High School. It was an hour bus ride to get to the other school. TyAnn was proud to be going along as a member of the "team." She sat quietly across the aisle from Robert on the bus.

Robert asked, "Are you all right, Tanny? You haven't said a word since we left."

"I'm a little scared. What if I make a mistake and Coach yells at me. He's always yelling at you guys."

Robert assured her, "You will do fine, and Coach Anderson will never yell at you."

She tried to smile.

Robert said, "Just because he is Coach Anderson now doesn't mean that he is not still our Uncle Bill."

TyAnn smiled at Robert and relaxed.

Robert took the court for the warm-ups. He looked around and thought, "This gym is huge compared to ours." The crowd roared as their team came out of the locker room and began their warm-up drills. Robert watched as several of the North Clay players dunked the ball. North Clay even had three African American players on the team. None of the players on the Hornets had ever played against boys of color before. Some of the seniors complained to Coach Anderson. Coach told them to be men and shut up and just play. Robert was the first to shake hands with the players on the other team as they gathered at center court for the jump ball to start the game.

After the rough start which found the Hornets trailing by eighteen points at halftime, the players had fought back. Point by point they cut the lead. Now with only five seconds left in the game they had the ball trailing by one point. Coach Anderson diagrammed the play which would hopefully free Robert for a shot from his favorite spot on the court.

"Boys, I'm proud of the way you've fought back. You have worked hard and played as a team. Nothing that happens in these last few seconds can change that." Coach stood in the middle as the team clasped hands. "Okay, on three. One. Two. Three. Hornets!"

The players hollered, then broke the huddle and took their spots on the court. Chip Hollins passed the ball inbounds to Robert, who was immediately double-teamed. Chip set a screen to free Robert. Somehow Robert managed to get away. He glanced at the clock. With one second on the clock he jumped as high as he could. He got off a shot from the top of the key. The ball bounced off the front of the rim and against the backboard. It settled on the front of the rim. It seemed about to drop into the basket when inexplicably it fell off to the side. The Hornets lost the game. Even though they came up one point short, Coach Anderson remained proud of his boys, He knew that if they could play this well against a large school like North Clay, they would do fine against teams in their conference.

Mom and Dad were disappointed that his last second shot didn't go in, but were proud of the way Robert played. TyAnn wanted to ride on the bus on the way home, and since it was Friday night, Mom gave her permission. On the way home she sat with Robert, and tried to console him as he cried because he missed the shot.

"Even Jerry West misses a shot once in a while," TyAnn said, knowing that was his favorite player.

Robert finally cheered up enough to smile at her and pull on her ponytail. "Yeah, I guess so, but he doesn't miss many when the game is on the line.

The Hornets didn't lose another game until Christmastime

when they played in a holiday tournament. They lost to a very strong team from South Warsaw in the championship game. They trailed all throughout the game and ended up losing by ten points. They didn't feel too bad about it later when South Warsaw ended up going to state. The Hornets didn't lose any games at home all year.

TyAnn teased Bubby, "You guys won all those games because you had good managers on the bench."

Robert teased her back, "You're absolutely right. Steve is the best manager any team could have!"

"What about me?"

"Oh yeah! I forgot you are a manager, too."

When state tournament time came around, their old nemesis, the Mount Trenton Wildcats soundly defeated the Hornets. The Wildcats had won the regional tournament for the last twenty years in a row. Robert ended up leading the team in scoring by averaging over fifteen points a game. With only four losses for the whole year, it was one of the team's best seasons ever.

Chapter Thirteen

When summer break arrived, Dad had a surprise for the family. They had saved up enough money to go on vacation. Dad sat in his chair in the living room and talked to the kids, "Mom and I have decided we have enough money saved to go on vacation for two weeks. We thought we would go somewhere we visited a few years ago." Dad grinned at Mom. They had gone there on their honeymoon. "How would you like to go to Smoky Mountain National Park?"

TyAnn screamed, "Yes! Yes!" then asked Dad, "What is Smoky Park?"

Dad laughed and explained, "It's a national park down in Tennessee. It's huge. There are mountains and trees everywhere. I think it got it's name because of the fog. It makes it look like smoke."

"I hope Charger doesn't get lost in the woods."

"You know Charger will have to stay at the farm while we are on vacation, Tanny."

She thought about it for a moment. She didn't know if she could survive being away from Charger for two whole weeks. "I suppose so. She will miss me while I'm gone, though!"

TyAnn was excited to go, even though Charger had to stay behind.

TyAnn rode along with Dad when they took Charger out to Uncle Charlie and Aunt Mary's farm.

TyAnn knelt in front of her as she left instructions. "Charger, you be a good doggie and don't run off. I will be back soon, and I'll tell you all about our vacation in the mountains."

Charger seemed to understand TyAnn. She started running around the farm checking everything out. She chased a couple of squirrels up a tree.

David watched and told Charger, "Good girl! You can chase all the squirrels and rabbits you want out here, Charger."

After Dad and TyAnn left, Charger followed David all around the farm and didn't stray too far from his side.

The Benjamin family set off for their vacation. While on the road to the national park, Robert settled in for the long ride and began reading a new book. TyAnn was too wound up to simply sit back and read. She watched the scenery as they traveled south through Illinois, then Kentucky.

"When are we going to be there?" TyAnn asked Mom.

"Not until tomorrow, dear," Mom answered.

That night they stayed in a motel. TyAnn had never done that before. "Look, Mom, they have a swimming pool. Can Bubby and I go swimming?" she asked excitedly. "I've never been swimming anywhere but Grandpa's pond."

"We went swimming in Mount Trenton one time when we were younger," Robert said.

"We did? I don't remember that."

"You were pretty young, Tanny."

TyAnn had a great time in the pool with Robert, and they raced each other from one end to the other. At the end of the day, she was exhausted and fell asleep almost immediately.

In the morning they had breakfast in the fancy restaurant next to the motel called Howard Johnson's.

"Mom, look at all the different things they have on the menu. This is way better than eating at Kresge's back in Millstown. I think I'll try everything."

"TyAnn, I do believe you should just order one thing," Mom cautioned her.

"Bubby, what are you getting?"

"I'm going to get bacon and eggs with wheat toast."

"Then I think I'll have blueberry pancakes. I do like bacon though." TyAnn hinted, hoping Robert would share with her.

"If there's enough, I'll share my bacon with you, Tanny."

"Thank you, Bubby," she said as she smiled at him.

Later that day, they finally arrived at their destination. They had rented a cabin in the woods for the week.

"It's just like being in the woods back home!" TyAnn exclaimed.

She followed Dad and Robert out back. "See those! I don't think we have mountains like that back home," Dad said.

"Whoa! No, we don't. Can Bubby and I go hiking in the mountains?"

"Maybe, but they are not as close as you might think. I'm

41

sure there are plenty of hiking trails which are closer," Dad mentioned.

"Maybe I will get you lost in the woods and leave you for the bears and wolves," Robert teased.

"Ha! Ha! Aren't you the funny guy?" She looked around nervously as she heard something moving through the woods. She relaxed as she spotted a deer and a fawn, as they trotted across the clearing at the back of the cabin.

They looked forward to spending the week hiking through the woods and meadows of Smoky Mountain National Park. TyAnn received quite a surprise one day when they saw deer as tame as cows in an area called Cades Cove. At twelve years old and still a complete tomboy, she tried to keep up with Robert and everything he did. Including one morning as they hiked in the park. They heard something on the trail up ahead. Robert looked and saw a bear. He didn't want to scare his sister, so he whispered, "Don't move, Tanny. Be quiet. There is a bear on the trail just ahead."

"A real bear, Bubby?" She took his hand and hid behind him. She peeked around Robert to see the bear. They kept as still as possible as they watched for a few seconds. The bear continued on his way into the woods, and they decided to head back to the cabin.

When they got close, TyAnn made a beeline back and yelled to Mom as soon as she saw her. "We saw a bear in the woods. A real bear!"

"What were you doing?" Dad asked.

Robert said, "We were on the same trail as yesterday, and we came across a brown bear crossing the trail."

Dad asked TyAnn, "Were you scared?"

TyAnn replied, "Nope! Not at all. Bubby was with me, and besides, I could outrun Bubby, and the bear would get him instead of me!"

Robert grabbed her and threw her over his shoulder.

"I'm going to take you back to the woods and feed you to the bears!" he teased.

"Put me down," TyAnn screamed.

He unceremoniously dumped her in a pile of leaves and

held her there. TyAnn asked him sternly, "You wouldn't really feed me to the bears, would you?"

"Of course not," Robert replied. "You would give the bears an upset stomach."

She pouted and threw some leaves at him. "Brothers are a pain in the butt, but I love you anyway."

"I love you, too, Tanny!" Robert replied, "Even if you are a girl!"

They made nightly use of the fire ring in back of the cabin. Robert and Dad bought some firewood from a local man and built campfires every night. TyAnn roasted marshmallows and even hot dogs. As the whole family sat around the fire at night, TyAnn was amazed at how many stars were visible in the clear night sky.

"Can you identify the different constellations, TyAnn?" Dad asked.

She looked up at the sky. "I can tell which one is the Big Dipper, but that's all."

Dad pointed out different constellations to her.

"I still don't think they look like anything but stars. I guess I don't have a good imagination."

The week flew by, and before TyAnn was ready it was time to leave.

Dad told Mom, "We have enough money left from our vacation budget to stay in motels for a couple nights."

They loaded up the car and headed back home. They made a few stops along the way in different state parks that looked interesting. It took three days to get home.

As soon as they finished unloading the car, TyAnn asked Dad, "Can we go get Charger now, please? I'm sure she knows I'm home, and is just waiting to be picked up."

"Okay, sweetie. Give me a few minutes to relax, then we will go get Charger."

"Thank you, Daddy!"

Dad drove out to Uncle Charlie's and as soon as he stopped the car, TyAnn jumped out and called, "Charger! I'm here! Where are you?"

TyAnn heard Charger bark, then saw her come running out of the woods. TyAnn got down on her knees as Charger ran toward her. Charger knocked TyAnn over, and started licking her face as she wagged her tail furiously. David walked out of the woods and saw TyAnn.

"I suppose you want to take Charger home now?"

"Hi, David! Of course I want to take her home now. Was she a good girl for you?"

"She was a good girl, but I could tell she missed you," David said.

"Did you miss me, Charger? Did you enjoy running all over the farm and the woods? We can go home now, and I'll tell you all about our trip."

Chapter Fourteen

The new school year started, and TyAnn looked forward to basketball season as much as Robert. When the girls played basketball in gym class, she proved, without a doubt, who was the best player. She was still such a tomboy, and liked to play ball with the boys whenever she could. She got straight A's in school, just like her brother, and tried to impress him with her knowledge. Robert pretended not to be impressed by his little sister, but secretly he was very proud of her. Robert had grown another inch this year and had gotten stronger. His cousins David and Chuck grew also. David stood six-two and Chuck towered above him—a whole inch taller at six-three. They would be the starting forwards on this years team. With three sophomores in the starting lineup, Coach Anderson didn't know what to expect.

One fall day TyAnn came outside to watch Robert playing ball in the backyard with David, Chuck and some other friends.

"Can I play, too? I won't get in the way, I promise."

"Okay, you can play, Tanny, but you need to be careful and stay on the outside of the court," Robert said.

The boys were so much bigger and stronger than her now, so she had to be careful. One time, as she reached for a loose ball, David bumped into her and hit her head with his elbow. She collapsed to the ground—out cold. Robert dashed over to her because she didn't move.

"David, run in the house and get Mom!"

David sprinted in the house, and Mom came running out.

"What happened?"

"It was an accident. David didn't see Tanny, and he hit the side of her head."

"I'm really sorry. I didn't mean to hit her."

"I know. It was an accident."

By this time, TyAnn was groaning. She woke up and saw Robert over her. "What happened?" she asked.

"You hit David's elbow with your head," Robert joked.

David caught on. "Ow! My elbow is killing me. I think you broke it, Ty."

"You guys are teasing. I'm calling a foul on whoever hit

45

me," TyAnn said.

After Mom was sure she was all right, the boys began playing again, but TyAnn was not allowed to play real games with them anymore. TyAnn still shot baskets with her brother and cousins, but could only play real games in gym class with the other girls.

The basketball season arrived, and the Hornets got off to a good start. They won nine out of their first ten games—losing only to South Warsaw by three points in a close game. The three sophomores continued to surprise Coach Anderson by holding their own against more experienced teams. The other two starters on the team were seniors who provided solid, if unspectacular, play. They knew their roles and didn't try to do more than their talent allowed.

A new student transferred into school midway through the first semester and joined the team for the last part of the season. Roger Stephens, was also a sophomore—six-six and well built— not a skinny kid like the senior who had been their starting center. Roger had grown up on a farm and had the muscles to prove it. Coach Anderson thought the future sure looked bright for his team. The season ended with another loss to Mount Trenton in the regional finals, but this time the Hornets kept the final score closer. They only lost by thirteen points.

TyAnn still enjoyed her role with team, and even served as a cheerleader for the junior high Warriors. Her natural athletic ability, and her small size, made her a natural for the tumbling part of cheering. On April 10, a special event happened in TyAnn's life. She became a teenager.

Robert teased her, "You still look like you're ten. I don't think you're really a teenager. I think Mom and Dad forgot what year you were really born."

"You can tease me all you want, but I know I'm a real teenager," she replied as she made a face at him.

Chapter Fifteen

After the school year ended, Robert and TyAnn spent a whole month at the farm helping Grandma and Grandpa. Robert helped in the fields and other jobs with Grandpa. Grandpa was getting too old to take care of the whole farm by himself, so Robert was a big help to him. The three Tomanek brothers, August, Charlie and Frank, lived on nearby farms. The oldest brother, August, who everyone called Gus, worked his farm with his two sons, Dwayne and Ed. David Tomanek helped his father, Charlie, on the farm because his older brothers, Steve and Mark, were in the army. Chuck Tomanek and his step-brothers, Jimmy and Andy Wilson, helped their father, Frank Tomanek, on his smaller farm. The oldest step-brother, Tom Wilson, had joined the army, also.

TyAnn helped Grandma with cooking and also in the yard. Grandma loved her flowers, and taught TyAnn about the different kinds and how to take care of them. Robert and TyAnn both helped in the vegetable garden and with the canning and preserving of food. When they got a chance, both kids still went swimming in the large pond. TyAnn liked to work on her tan and listened to her transistor radio. She brought a blanket to sit on in the sandy area off to the north side of the pond.

One day the boys decided to go swimming in the pond. Since it was such a hot day, the boys decided to strip to their underwear. TyAnn didn't know and wandered down to the pond herself to work on her tan and listen to her radio. She heard the boys playing in the pond but didn't pay any attention to them. She relaxed by the pond and took off her shirt and shorts and had on her bathing suit. The boys heard her radio and noticed her working on her tan. The boys looked up at the tall bank at the west end of the pond.

Chuck told Robert, "You can climb up the bank and grab our shorts and toss them down to us."

Robert decided to take a chance and climbed out of the pond. He grabbed the shorts and threw them down to the boys. It only took three seconds. TyAnn didn't pay them any attention as she read a book. All the boys left except Robert.

Robert came over and sat next to TyAnn. He wondered if

she saw anything, but TyAnn didn't say anything about what the boys were doing. Robert assumed she didn't see anything.

"I'm going back to the house to get a pop to drink. Do you want something?" Robert asked.

"A cold Coke would be great, and bring me some of Grandma's cookies and a pillow and another towel."

Robert asked her sarcastically, "Anything else, Your Highness?"

She looked at him and replied with a smile, "Oh, I will think of more for you to do, unless you want me to tell Mom what you were wearing in the pond."

Robert knew he had been had. "You saw didn't you?"

TyAnn smiled and told him, "I saw your underwear when you climbed out and now you are my servant."

"We'll see about that," Robert quipped. He marched off to get what she demanded and soon returned. "Anything else, Your Highness," Robert asked in a high-brow tone.

She smiled and dismissed him with a wave of her hand. "That will be all for now."

She thought about it for awhile and told Robert, "I want to go swimming, too!"

TyAnn got up and hustled to the pond and jumped in. "Are you gonna join me?" she hollered.

"Yeah, but I'm keeping my shorts on this time." He joined her in the deep end of the pond.

"Maybe we shouldn't tell Grandma we were swimming," TyAnn said.

"Good idea," Robert said as he spat out some water. "She doesn't like it when we swim in the pond."

"It will be our secret, Bubby," TyAnn said as she had fun in the pond.

Ten minutes later, they got out of the pond.

"Were you looking at me?" TyAnn asked as she dried off and got dressed.

"Oh, Tanny, I didn't look at your pretty face, or any other part of you as you were getting out of the pond," Robert said as he tossed a stone into the pond.

"Really?"

"Really!"

"So you think I'm pretty then, huh?"

Robert made a face and said, "No, I just said that to make you happy."

She kicked his shin, and they were ready to go back to the house.

"I'm still telling Mom!" TyAnn yelled as she ran away from Robert. He chased her and caught her as she was climbing over the wooden fence gate. He threw her over his shoulder and began to tickle her sides.

She cried out, "Okay, I won't tell."

"Cry uncle?"

"I give up!" TyAnn squealed.

Robert let her down.

"Fingers crossed!" TyAnn yelled as she scooted away again.

Robert shook his head and gave up. Grandma came out the back door and saw TyAnn running toward her.

"Supper is ready, honey. Where is your brother?"

"He was right behind me a minute ago. He was trying to tickle me, Grandma. Will you make him stop?"

"I'm sure he was just teasing you. He loves you, you know?"

"I know, Grandma."

After supper was done, TyAnn helped with the dishes. Grandma had a faraway look on her face.

"What are you thinking about Grandma?" TyAnn asked her softly.

"Oh, child, I was thinking about something that happened to Grandpa and myself a long, long time ago," Grandma replied wistfully.

"Can you tell me about it?" TyAnn asked hopefully.

"Let's sit on the porch swing, and I will tell you a story."

"Come on, Bubby. Grandma is going to tell us a story," TyAnn said as she pulled Robert along with her. TyAnn sat next to Grandma on the swing and Robert sat in a rocking chair beside them.

"It happened a long time ago," Grandma began, then paused as she closed her eyes. "It was a cold rainy morning in July as Grandpa and I made our way to Clark Street dock along the

Chicago River."

"How old were you, Grandma?"

"I was nineteen years old, and we had only been married a few months. It was the day of the fifth annual Western Electric Company picnic to be held in Michigan City, Indiana. Over 7000 tickets were sold for the event, and three ships were chartered and waiting at the Clark Street dock. The Theodore Roosevelt, the Petoskey and the Eastland."

"I've heard of those ships," Robert said.

"Be quiet, Bubby, I want to hear Grandma tell this story," TyAnn said as she stuck out her tongue at him.

"Many of the employees going with us on the Eastland were our Bohemian friends from Cicero. For many of us it was our only holiday of the year, as we were too poor to travel anywhere. We looked forward to the trip with much anticipation. The ship started loading at around 6:30 in the morning and shortly afterward had reached its capacity. We boarded the Eastland with a couple of our friends. Many of the passengers went below."

"Was it really cold?" TyAnn asked.

"Sssh. Be quiet, Tanny."

"Now don't fight," Grandma said. "It was cold, so a lot of people went inside to get warm and escape the chilly morning air. Others stayed on the open top deck. Grandpa and I couldn't find any chairs so we went inside with our friends. There was a canoe race happening on the river and many people moved to the port side of the ship, away from the dock, to watch the canoes race by." Grandma paused for a moment. "Suddenly, and without any warning, the ship began to roll over. The ship rolled completely over on its side and I think it sank to the bottom of the river. All of the people on the decks were tossed in the river. We were inside a small room and the only way out was through a port hole. One of Grandpa's friends climbed out of the porthole and found a rope. He lowered the rope and this fat man started to climb out. I was so afraid that he would get stuck and we would all drown, but he eventually wiggled his way through the porthole, then the rest of us were able to climb out."

TyAnn stared at Grandma in amazement. Robert looked at Grandma mesmerized.

"We climbed out of the porthole and were picked up by a

50

small boat on the river. I can still remember the cries and screams of those who were dying."

Grandma stopped talking for a moment and had tears in her eyes. TyAnn held Grandma's hand until she stopped crying and could continue with her story.

"I remember people standing on a drawbridge looking down at us. I saw a young mother floating in the water holding on to a chair. She had her baby on the chair and they were rescued. So many people were killed, and we lost so many friends."

TyAnn looked at Grandma with tears in her eyes and hugged her tightly. Robert had heard the story from Mom before, but TyAnn never had. Grandma sat in her swing, quietly reflecting back on that day when the angel of death had visited the city of Chicago.

Chapter Sixteen

The next morning Grandma and Grandpa rose very early, as people who lived on a farm usually did. Grandpa always got out of bed first. He slept in a room at the back of the house. Grandma would get up after she heard him moving around. She made coffee for them and they had a chance to talk without any distractions.

Robert eventually got up and found Grandma making biscuits and gravy for breakfast and asked, "Morning, Grandma, that smells good. Where is TyAnn?"

"She had a bad dream last night and came in to my room."

Robert didn't remember a storm last night.

"I think my story about the Eastland upset her. She's still in my bed. Why don't you see if she's awake. Breakfast will be ready in a few minutes."

Robert quietly stepped into Grandma's room and saw TyAnn still asleep. He was about to leave when she called to him, "Bubby, I had a bad dream last night and got scared."

"I know. Grandma told me. Are you okay now?"

"I'm fine now, but I'm hungry."

"Well, then get your lazy butt out of bed and come and have breakfast. We have chores to do," Robert said as he pulled the covers off of her.

She threw a pillow at him, but missed.

TyAnn came into the kitchen and smelled the delicious aromas of Grandma's cooking. Biscuits and gravy, bacon and eggs, potato dumplings and sausage. She asked Grandma, "Why are you making so much for breakfast?"

"Have you forgotten, child? Today is the day everybody is coming over to help paint the barn."

"Oh, I forgot all about that. Mom and Dad are coming."

A short time later, all of her uncles and aunts pulled their cars into the barnyard and walked into the house. TyAnn went to her room and got dressed quickly. Mom and Dad arrived, and she hurried to see them.

She asked Mom, "Did you miss me?"

Mom answered, "Oh, were you gone?"

TyAnn hugged her and told her, "You know I've been gone, and I missed you."

"Of course, I missed you, sweetheart. I even missed your brother."

"You can take him back, if you want. He doesn't do much of anything around here to be helpful."

"I heard that," Robert answered back.

Grandma kept making more food and everybody ate way too much. Soon everybody was stuffed to the gills and Grandpa told them, "Now it is time for work. We have lots to do today."

The men headed out to the barn where Grandpa already had the paint, brushes and other supplies needed for the job ready and waiting. With all of the uncles and cousins helping the job didn't take long at all. The most difficult part was the section at each end. Dwayne and Ed climbed the tall ladders to reach the highest sections. TyAnn saw Coach Anderson and skipped over to him. She started to call him coach, but caught herself and said, "Hello, Uncle Bill," instead as she hugged him.

"Hello, TyAnn. I hear you and Robert have been staying with Grandma and Grandpa this summer."

"Yeah, we have! It's hard work sometimes, but I love being out here in the country."

TyAnn's job for the day was to make sure the men had plenty of water to drink. She did a good job, and Grandpa thanked her and hugged her tightly. Grandpa was usually not very demonstrative in his affection, but Grandma had told him about TyAnn's bad dream after hearing about the Eastland. Grandpa loved his only granddaughter very much, but didn't always know how to let her know. He had been a hard-working farmer for most of his life, and had built most of the farm buildings with his own two hands. TyAnn kissed Grandpa on the cheek and skipped merrily back to the house. Robert was watching, and, though he couldn't swear to it, he thought he saw a tear in Grandpa's eye.

After the men finished the barn, Grandpa told them that the corn crib needed painting. The men let out a collective groan.

Grandpa said, "You didn't think I was going to let you off so easy as that. Now let's get started on the corn crib, then maybe you can take a break for dinner."

"Come on, guys! At least the corn crib is not as tall."

"Yeah, and it's the same color as the barn."

Grandpa would never think of painting any of the out-buildings, or the house, any color other than white. Everyone moved over to the corn crib and they worked diligently to finish that building. Grandma came out to inspect the work. She looked over the buildings very carefully and pointed out a spot that someone missed.

"Look there!" she said. "Someone missed that spot. Now it needs to be fixed, or else everyone will see what a poor job has been done."

All the men looked at the area that Grandma had pointed out, but nobody else could see what she apparently could. TyAnn's father volunteered to climb back up the ladder and fix the area Grandma pointed to. Dad spent some time working on the "spot" until Grandma gave her approval.

Robert asked his Dad, "Did you really do anything to the place Grandma was pointing at?"

"No, I didn't have any more paint in my bucket," Dad answered. "But don't tell your grandmother." Robert laughed and nodded.

TyAnn wandered over to Grandpa's machine shop and opened the side door. Grandma saw her and told her for the thousandth time, "Don't go up in the loft because there is a Blue Racer snake up there."

"I won't, Grandma," TyAnn promised.

Grandma told Robert, "Go with your sister and make sure she is okay. I don't want her to climb up in that loft and get hurt."

Robert obeyed and followed TyAnn into the machine shop. He saw her climbing into the loft and hollered, "Tanny, what are you doing? You know Grandma doesn't want you climbing all over like one of the boys."

"I can climb up here just as easy as you 'boys' can, and I want to see this snake for myself," TyAnn hollered back as she climbed up to the loft. "I don't believe there has ever been a snake up here at all."

She climbed into the loft, and not one minute later Robert heard her scream, "Bubby!"

He raced over and quickly climbed up in the loft. He saw TyAnn standing against the wall pointing at something. Robert flew over to her and looked in the direction she pointed. Sure enough Grandma was right! There, as clear as day, was the largest snake he had ever seen. He grabbed TyAnn's arm and pulled her away from the snake.

"Climb back down and tell Dad about the snake."

"You can tell him. I'm outta here!"

He waited a minute, then followed her. He told Grandpa about the snake. Dad and Uncle Charlie hustled into the machine shop, climbed up to the loft with shovels and killed the snake. Even Grandma seemed surprised when Uncle Charlie brought the snake out into the barnyard for everyone to see.

Mom asked Grandma, "Did you really know that snake was up there?"

Grandma replied, "Well, I saw one up there twenty years ago, and figured there still might be snakes up there now."

"I bet you haven't been in that loft for twenty years!"

Grandma smiled and said, "Of course not, Emma. Don't you know there are snakes up there?"

Chapter Seventeen

After all the excitement about the snake and the hard work, everyone was hungry and ready for dinner. Although it was only one o'clock, it was time for dinner. Supper being the last meal of the day down on the farm. Grandma had another feast for everyone—plates of fried chicken, dumplings, mashed potatoes and homemade gravy and several different vegetables. Even apple and cherry pies for dessert. TyAnn was asked to tell her story about the snake for everyone.

Robert said, "Tanny was so brave and not afraid at all!"

Later, TyAnn told Robert, "I was not brave. I was so scared I thought I was going to wet my pants."

"But you didn't, and that was the main thing. You didn't run away like most girls would do."

"That's because I couldn't move my legs."

Robert smiled and poked her in the side.

After dinner Grandpa told the men, "Thank you very much for the hard work today. The barn and corn crib look twenty times better. I don't have anything else that needs to be finished today."

They were all relieved until Grandma said, "My chicken shed needs a new coat of paint, and there is a hole in the fence by the corn crib."

Grandpa said, "The chicken shed will have to wait until I can get more paint, and I fixed the hole in the fence yesterday."

Grandma told them, "Well, since you can't paint anymore, the brush needs to be cleared behind the shed and the yard needs to be mowed."

Grandpa and all the uncles and cousins were kept busy all afternoon by Grandma. As soon as they finished one job, Grandma found something else that needed attention. At the end of the day, the farm looked better than ever. While the men had been working outside, the women had been working inside. They had cleaned the whole house—top to bottom! They had been busy cooking for supper, also. When suppertime arrived, TyAnn was allowed to go first because of her ordeal with the snake. She stuck her tongue out at Robert to tease him. For supper they had everything left over from dinner and more potatoes, fried chicken, corn and more.

After supper that night, it was time to make homemade ice

cream—TyAnn's favorite dessert of all time. All of her uncles, and her Dad, had their own ice cream makers and everybody made a different flavor. TyAnn had a special job to help Dad make his ice cream. After the cranking got too hard, TyAnn stood on the bucket to stabilize it and enable Dad to finish the cranking. It seemed to take forever to her, but it only took half an hour. Then came the hardest part. They packed the ice cream with lots of ice, and had to wait until it was good and hard. Finally, Grandma inspected the ice cream and declared it to be ready. Aunt Mary had made a German chocolate cake because it was Uncle Charlie's favorite. There were four different flavors of ice cream to choose from banana, peach, strawberry and, of course, vanilla.

TyAnn asked Mom, "Can I have a little of each flavor, please?"

"Now why did I know you were going to ask for that, hmmmm?"

Mom gave her a spoonful of each flavor to try. Robert and David had a contest to see who could eat the most ice cream the fastest. Robert won but paid the price with a "brain-freeze." TyAnn was allowed to have another dish after everybody else had eaten at least one bowl. Grandma pulled out a chocolate cake that she forgotten about. Soon everyone was groaning again about eating way too much food.

Grandma chased the men outside, "Give us some room. We need to clean the kitchen and the dining room again. Go out on the porch and talk to each other."

"Can I help with anything, Grandma?" TyAnn asked.

"You've done enough work for the day, TyAnn. Why don't you go outside with your father and Robert and relax."

TyAnn gave Grandma a kiss. The men sat outside on the front porch and talked about growing up on the farm. TyAnn sat on the porch rail next to Robert and listened intently to all the stories. She enjoyed listening to the stories even if she had heard some of them before. Uncle Charlie liked to tell jokes and always made her laugh. Later, TyAnn started to get sleepy and rested her head against Robert's shoulder and fell asleep. He noticed and put his arm around her so she wouldn't fall off the railing. She woke up after a few minutes and looked up at Robert.

"You must be tired, Tanny. You fell asleep."

"I feel better now. Let's go down to the pond and listen to the birds and bugs."

All the younger cousins headed down to the pond. They sat on the bank and talked about school and basketball.

"I think we are going to beat Mount Trenton this year," TyAnn predicted.

"It would be nice to finally get past that team," Robert answered.

Soon Mom called for TyAnn and Robert to come back to the house.

"I'll race you to the house, Bubby."

TyAnn took off and Robert chased her. He caught her, of course, and grabbed her and threw her over his shoulder. He carried her to the front porch.

"Robert, you should put her down," Grandma said.

"It's all right, Grandma. I don't mind."

Mom said, "We are going home. Is there anything you need from the house?"

"I could use a couple more t-shirts and more socks." TyAnn looked at Robert, then whispered in Mom's ear, "I need some more underwear, too."

Mom nodded her head. TyAnn kissed Mom and Dad good night.

"Call me during the week so I know you are all right," Mom instructed her.

"I will," TyAnn said. She was exhausted, so she put on her pajamas and told Robert good night.

He teased her, "I know you asked Mom for more underwear, Tanny."

She answered by smacking his arm, "Did not!"

They were both too tired to tease each other anymore. They went to their rooms and fell asleep the moment their heads hit the pillow.

The month on the farm passed by quickly, and the kids were back home. Robert had worked very hard while on the farm and gained some needed upper body strength. TyAnn had learned how hard Grandma worked. She now knew how to make apple pies and how to cook fried chicken and other of Grandma's specialties. She tried to be a better helper to Mom with the housework. Mom noticed and hugged her and thanked her for her extra effort. TyAnn was even nicer to Robert and he wondered what had gotten into her. One day he really noticed TyAnn and could see a change. She had changed from a little girl and was turning into a young lady. As they were sitting on the couch one night, Robert told her how pretty she looked. TyAnn looked at him waiting for the punch line, but Robert didn't tease her. He was serious.

She moved closer to him and whispered, "Thanks, Bubby."

Chapter Eighteen

School had started for Robert's junior year. Working behind the scenes on the different committees to organize the Junior Carnival kept him busier than ever. TyAnn was in eighth grade already. Mom couldn't believe how fast they were growing up. Mom looked at TyAnn and still saw her little baby. TyAnn didn't look any older than ten to Mom and Dad. She still usually wore her hair in a ponytail, but had started wearing dresses more often to school. Late in the fall the town heard the news that President Kennedy had been shot and killed.

Basketball season arrived at last. Robert, David, Chuck and Roger were back for their junior years. They were joined in the starting lineup by Kevin Ambuehl, another junior. Roger had grown another inch and added more muscle to his frame. David was six-four and so was Chuck. Robert was now six-two and stronger than ever. Kevin was the shortest member of the bunch at five-ten. Kevin had been a substitute the two previous years and had almost as much experience as the other boys. Coach Anderson had some lofty goals for this year's squad. The gym was sold out for every game before the season even started. Somehow they managed to shoehorn five hundred people into the small gym. Some of the local townspeople wanted to build a bigger gym, but the school district didn't have the money. The boys played together as a team, and over the course of the year, each of the starters led the team in scoring in at least one game. Robert set a new school record when he scored forty-four points in a big win against North Clay. The squad went through the whole season undefeated. They were almost defeated at South Warsaw, but Robert made two free throws at the end of the game to send them into overtime. They held South Warsaw scoreless in overtime and won by six points.

In the regional tournament they won their first two games, and once again faced Mount Trenton in the finals.

"Coach, I really think we're going to beat them this year," Principal Woods told him.

"This might be our best chance in quite a while. I can't remember Mount Trenton losing twelve games in a year before. I

60

know the competition they play is much tougher than ours, but still, I truly believe we are a better team."

This time the Hornets started off the game with a surprise. They pressed Mount Trenton all over the court and kept the pace frenetic. Coach Anderson knew his boys were in the best shape of their lives and could run all night long. The strategy worked to their favor, and at the start of the fourth quarter, Kinmundy Junction had a three point lead. The fourth quarter was the most stressful eight minutes of Coach Anderson's life. Everybody in the building seemed to be a bundle of nerves. The hometown Mount Trenton fans were restless. Even the referees sensed something special was happening. The only person in the building who seemed calm was Robert Benjamin. He had been dreaming of this for most of his life. Going into the last thirty seconds. Kinmundy Junction was still leading, but only by one point now. Robert tipped a pass and there was a scramble for the loose ball. One of the referees called a foul on Kevin Ambuehl—his fifth foul of the game. Brent Gentry, a sophomore, replaced him. The Mount Trenton player made both free throws to give them a one point lead. Robert brought the ball up court, faked a pass to the left wing, moved to his right and calmly made a jumper from just above the free throw line to give Kinmundy Junction a one point lead. Mount Trenton called their last timeout. Neither team had a timeout left. Mount Trenton worked the ball inside and their big center made a fall-away jumper to give the Wildcats a one point lead. Roger was called for his fifth foul. His younger brother, Randy, replaced him. Only five seconds remained in the game. Mount Trenton missed the free throw, and Robert grabbed the rebound. He looked at the clock. He knew he had plenty of time. He passed the ball up court to Brent Gentry and sprinted for the other end. Brent passed him the ball back, and Robert had time to take his favorite shot. At the top of his jump, a Mount Trenton player hit Robert's arm and knocked him down. Robert got his shot off just before the final buzzer sounded. Though confident he had made the basket, he waited to hear the referee's whistle to call the obvious foul. While he lay on the floor, the ball hit the back of the rim, bounced into the air, came down, hung on the rim for a heartbeat, then slipped off to the side. Robert now thought he must make both free throws to win the game, but something was wrong. The Mount Trenton players were celebrating as their fans rushed onto the court. Robert looked at the referee closest to him, but the referee turned his head and scurried away. Robert looked over at Coach Anderson, who appeared totally stunned with both hands raised in the air. Coach knew that both referees saw the obvious foul, but seemed afraid to make the call against the hometown team. The Hornets were heartbroken. Roger felt like punching someone. Randy Stephens and Brent Gentry waited near the free throw line. David and Chuck kept looking for the referees. The other players sat on the bench waiting for instructions. They felt sure the referees would clear the crowd from the floor so Robert could shoot his free throws. But nothing happened. The Mount Trenton team kept celebrating with their fans. Mom and Dad stood up from their seats. They couldn't believe how their team had been robbed. TyAnn hustled out to the court to console her Bubby. Coach Anderson shook hands with the the Mount Trenton coach.

"I'm sorry about what happened, Bill. It was an obvious foul and should have been called. I'll write a report, and maybe we can see to it that those referees are dealt with."

"It's all part of the game. Good luck the rest of the way."

Coach Anderson strode onto the court to pick Robert up from the floor.

Robert could only say, "I'm sorry, Uncle Bill. I missed the shot and ruined the season."

Uncle Bill said, "We never would had made it this far without you. Next year will be different."

Coach Anderson addressed the team in the locker room, "I want you to keep your heads up and be proud of what you accomplished this year. I don't want to hear any complaining about referees or bad calls. We lost the game and that's what happened. We will work even harder next year, and not put ourselves in a position to let one bad call from a referee make any difference in the outcome of a game."

Later that night, a very quiet and sad group of boys rode the bus back to Kinmundy Junction. It seemed the whole town met the team at the edge of town and used the fire truck to escort them back to the school. The town's only squad car was in the shop getting fixed after an accident.

Coach addressed the crowd, "I am so proud of these boys

and how hard they worked the whole season. The whole town should be proud of them! I know we came up short once again, but next year we will work even harder. I promise you that!"

Coach never once mentioned the non-call that cost them the game. Only his wife knew the pain he felt.

The following Monday the school honored the team with a pep rally. Coach Anderson presented all of the players awards for the outstanding year. He gave a speech and at the conclusion announced, "Now it's time for baseball, and I expect you guys to work just as hard on the ball diamond as you did in the gym."

In the locker room, Coach hung a new sign on the wall. It had four simple words on it. "Play Like A Champion." It became their motto for the next year.

TyAnn was disconsolate for a week after the game. Coach Anderson brightened everyone's spirits when he took the whole team to watch the state finals at the University of Illinois.

"Take a good look around, guys. Next year this will be us playing in the Assembly Hall for the state title," Kevin Ambuehl said.

Robert high-fived him, then added, "As hard as we worked this year, next year I'm going to double my efforts. We are just as good as any team in the state. I don't care how big a school they have. You can only play five players at a time, and we are going to be the best five players in the state."

TyAnn went to the games and was awed by the new building where the Fighting Illini played.

"This is the biggest place I have ever seen, Bubby! It's so huge. I think we could fit the whole town in here."

"Maybe half the town, Tanny."

They watched the games, and ended up rooting for the team from Covington to win. The Cornhuskers made it to the finals, but were defeated by Reedsburg High School in a close game.

On the way home Robert told TyAnn, "Next year you will be a cheerleader, and you will be leading cheers in that big building. Everyone will be watching you, so you better practice hard on your routines, okay!"

"Okay, Bubby. I will."

Chapter Nineteen

Robert had a lead role in the junior class play. They were doing a production of the famous play by Tennessee Hummingway *A Night In A Small Town.* Robert played the part of Rufus T. Driftwood, the main male character. David and Chuck had large roles in the play, also. Laurie Roland played Mrs. Dumont, the lead female character. TyAnn discovered that Robert had a crush on Laurie and she teased him about her mercilessly.

Robert finally got up the nerve to ask Laurie on a date. He took her to Millstown to watch a movie, then brought her back home—big mistake! As soon as Robert and Laurie sat on the living room couch, TyAnn plopped down between them. TyAnn asked Laurie, "Where did you guys go? Did he kiss you? Are you going to go out with him again? Do you think his ears look funny?"

Robert could stand only so much. He grabbed TyAnn's arm, pulled her into her bedroom, then tossed her on her bed, "I'm warning you. Don't move, or else I will tickle you to death. Do you understand?"

"I'm not afraid of you," she stuck out her tongue at him to prove her point.

"You better be afraid, be very afraid."

She smiled at Bubby, and he smiled back at her. Robert knew that she would be listening at the door to everything he told Laurie. Robert and Laurie sat on the couch and talked for awhile, until she needed to get home. Robert took her home but wasn't gone long, since Laurie lived only a few blocks away.

When Robert came back, he went to his room and stretched out on the bed. TyAnn came running into his room and jumped on the bed. She wanted to hear all about Bubby's first date. She sat beside him and bounced up and down with anticipation.

"Tell me, tell me!" TyAnn cried in an animated voice. "I want to hear all about it. Did you kiss her good night? Does she like you? Are you going to take her to the prom?"

TyAnn was so intense as she goaded Robert into telling her every detail of his night.

Robert said, "Okay, I'll tell you about the date. Just settle down. You have to promise not to tell anyone, all right?"

"I promise, cross my heart!" TyAnn solemnly swore.

Robert said, "We went to a show in Millstown, and we held hands in the theater. I kissed her good night on her front porch. Now does that satisfy you?"

TyAnn screamed in her loudest voice, "Mom! Mom! Robert kissed Laurie."

Robert sat up and pushed TyAnn down on the bed and put his hand over her mouth and warned her, "You are going to get it. I am going to tickle you to death right now. You promised not to tell anyone."

Robert began to tickle her as she cried out for Mom over and over. TyAnn laughed so hard, her sides started hurting.

Mom came into the room. "What is all this commotion about?"

Robert let up for a moment, and TyAnn blurted out, "Bubby kissed Laurie and he loves her."

Robert answered, "I did not say I loved her. I just kissed her good night."

Mom told them both to behave and walked away smiling. TyAnn continued to tease Bubby by blowing kisses at him and making faces.

"Tanny, you are going to pay big time for this. One of these days you will go on a date, and I will make your life miserable and embarrass you to death."

"I'm never going to go out with boys and certainly will never kiss one. Boys are icky and gross!" TyAnn exclaimed as she struggled to escape.

Most of the cast members suffered a bit of stage fright on the night of the play. Robert suffered more than most. The guys in the cast arrived early. Robert found a basketball and shot baskets to relax, it worked. Mrs. Sheffield, who taught English, directed the play. She held a final meeting and told them, "Now I want you to go out there and break a leg."

"Mrs. Sheffield, Coach Anderson will be awfully mad at us if we all break our legs. He expects us to win the state basketball championship next year." Once again Kevin used his humor to relax everyone.

TyAnn helped out the night of the play by selling tickets. She told everyone to pay close attention to the leading characters.

Just before the curtain opened, TyAnn rushed to her seat on the front row. The play was a big success despite one member of the audience trying to distract the lead characters by blowing kisses at them throughout the performance.

Robert asked Laurie to the prom in spite of TyAnn's constant teasing. The night of the prom found Robert dressed in his tuxedo nervously waiting while Mom took pictures. TyAnn had been warned by Mom to behave or else. She sat quietly on the couch watching her Bubby, sticking out her tongue and making kissing gestures at him whenever Mom was not looking. Mom made Robert promise to bring Laurie over for pictures before they headed down to the school. Even though the school and Laurie's home were only a few blocks apart, Robert had the family car for the night. Robert drove over to pick up Laurie and after pictures at her house, brought her back home for another session of pictures. TyAnn was on her best behavior and didn't even tease Robert or Laurie.

TyAnn told Robert before they left, "Bubby, you will be the most handsome boy at the prom."

"Oh, thanks," Robert replied dryly as he waited for the punch line.

"Even if you have funny looking ears!" TyAnn teased as she escaped to her room.

The students had spent many hours decorating the gym to look like a Hawaiian beach. If Robert used all his imagination, he thought it actually looked like a beach, but definitely not Hawaii. He danced with Laurie as the band, Fridays At Five, played for the evening. Soon the night was over, and by one o'clock Robert had Laurie home. Her parents had insisted she not stay for the post prom activities. He kissed her good night and returned home. He changed out of his tuxedo and got comfortable in his room. He heard a quiet knock on his door and whispered, "Come on in, Tanny."

He knew she had been waiting up to hear all the details about his night. She sat on his bed and listened patiently as Robert told her all about the prom. When he mentioned kissing Laurie good night, he expected Tanny to tease him, but she surprised him by just looking happy for him.

He said, "When you are older, some boy is going to want to take you to the prom."

"I won't go unless he is as nice and handsome as you. If he can play basketball, that would be a point in his favor," she as she surprised him with a kiss on his cheek before she jumped off the bed and walked into her room. Robert put his hand to his cheek thinking about how his baby sister was growing up. "It won't be too long before you start going on dates, Tanny."

Chapter Twenty

TyAnn graduated from junior high in June. She had the best grades of anyone in the class. Straight A's! Dad had always offered a dollar for every 'A' the kids got on their report card, but if they got anything lower than an 'A,' it would cost them five dollars. Robert made it through junior high with only three 'B's' on his report card. TyAnn had done even better. Now Dad had to pay up, "I guess I will have to go to the bank and take out a loan to pay you, honey!"

TyAnn smiled and held out her hand for her money. Dad counted it out for her.

"Thanks, Daddy. Now I'm going to the bank and putting this into my savings account."

"Aren't you going to spend any of it, Ty?" Robert asked.

"I suppose I could use some of the money to buy supper for everyone tonight."

"All right! I want the biggest steak they have."

Mom told TyAnn, "You don't have to buy us supper, dear. You should save your money. Your father will buy supper tonight, and Robert can even have his steak."

Everyone piled in the car, and they headed to Millstown. Mom had promised to buy a new dress for TyAnn. It didn't take too long to arrive in Millstown, and Dad found a parking space close to the Steiner Dress Shoppe.

"Are you coming in, Robert?" Mom asked.

"Do I have to?"

"No, you don't have to, but aren't you interested in what your sister gets?"

"I suppose I could force myself to watch. As long as she doesn't try on every dress in the place."

Robert tried to act excited for TyAnn because she had never had a dress from here before. They were rather expensive, but this was a special gift.

Inside the store Dad and Robert found chairs where they sat to watch. It only took fifteen minutes for Mom and TyAnn to find three dresses for her to try on. To Robert it seemed more like an hour, though. Dad passed the time reading his newspaper. TyAnn went into the dressing room and tried on the first dress. She came out to let Mom see. Dad looked up from his paper and noticed right away.

"That dress is too short! I can see your legs."

"Daddy! You will be able to see my legs in any dress I wear. In case you haven't noticed, girls don't wear dresses that come down to the floor anymore."

"Maybe you should try on the next one, honey," Mom said.

TyAnn tried on dress number two. This one came down to her knees but it didn't fit her right in the shoulders. Dress number three was just right! Even Robert agreed that TyAnn looked very pretty in this dress. It was not as short as the first dress and fit her perfectly.

"Do you like this one, honey?" Mom asked.

"Daddy, do you like it?"

"I think it looks perfect on you, Ty."

"We'll take it," Mom told the saleslady.

TyAnn changed out of the dress and back into her jeans. Dad smiled at her as she sat next to him.

"You look so pretty in your new dress, baby."

"Thank you, Daddy. I'm only gonna wear it on very special occasions."

"Are we gonna eat now?" Robert asked. "I'm starvin'."

"Yes, we can go now," Mom said as she looked at the price tag on a new purse.

There was a place in Millstown where Mom and Dad had only been once. It was too expensive for regular visits—Albert's Steak House. They had the best steaks in the county according to most customers. Dad and Robert had New York strip steaks while Mom and TyAnn had filet mignon. After they had finished their meals, everyone was stuffed, except Robert.

The waiter asked, "Can I interest anyone in dessert tonight?"

"No, thanks, we are going to make homemade ice cream tonight. That's the best dessert in the world!" TyAnn told the waiter.

He appeared unimpressed with her idea of a great dessert.

On the way home Robert teased TyAnn about her comment to the waiter.

"I don't care what kind of fancy dessert they have there. I

would rather have Daddy's ice cream. Besides, did you see how much a slice of cake cost?"

"Yeah, or a piece of pie a la mode. That's why I didn't order anything. What a rip!"

Everyone pitched in to help with the ice cream, and, after it had been in the freezer long enough, Mom pulled it out to inspect it.

"Come and get it!"

TyAnn nearly trampled Robert in her haste to get to the kitchen first. Soon nearly the whole half gallon of homemade ice cream had disappeared.

TyAnn told Mom and Dad, "That was the best ice cream I have ever had!"

"Thank you, honey. I'm glad you enjoyed all three bowls."

TyAnn smiled and stuck her tongue out at Robert.

In the summer before his senior year, Robert started getting swamped with letters from colleges. They were trying to recruit him to play basketball. Recruiters from schools large and small stopped by the house and talked to Mom and Dad. Robert told them that he had his mind made up already, but they continued to pursue him. Robert had known for several years that he would enroll at Southern Illinois University in Carbondale. Robert refused the recruiters offers to visit their school because he didn't want to waste his time, or theirs. He finally told TyAnn, "Will you answer the phone and tell everyone to stop calling and bothering me."

"Okay, but it will cost you."

"All right. I don't care what it costs. It will be worth it not to have to deal with everyone."

TyAnn did and was soon answering the phone like this, "This is the Benjamin residence. Robert is going to SIU, so leave him alone!"

She answered the phone several times a day using that line. She was getting as tired of the harassment as Robert and answered the phone for the fifth time in twenty minutes.

"He's going to SIU, so leave us alone and don't ever call again!"

She was about to hang up when she heard Grandma's voice.

"Honey, it's Grandma."

"Oh, I'm sorry, Grandma. I didn't know it was you. We have been getting so many calls from recruiters. I assumed this was another one of those."

"I wanted to tell Robert that the coach from Kansas was here earlier today, and Grandpa chased him away."

"Good for Grandpa! That coach has been here three times, and we don't even let him in the door anymore."

Chapter Twenty-One

Mom and Dad were sitting on the couch one evening after supper. "Emma, what would you think about going with me to Colorado. I know it might be kinda boring during the day while I'm in class, but we would have our evenings together."

"I've always wanted to see the Rocky Mountains. Can we afford it?"

"The insurance company is paying my expenses, and we have enough in savings to spend a week on our own. It could be like a second honeymoon."

"What about the kids?"

"Robert can look after TyAnn, and your parents are close. Charlie and Mary could keep an eye on them, too."

"It would give them a chance to show how responsible they can be. TyAnn is always asking to help me cook. This would give her a time to learn how to cook without me watching."

Dad had to spend two weeks in June in Denver, Colorado, taking a class for the insurance company he still worked for in the summer. Mom felt apprehensive about leaving the kids behind.

In the morning Mom talked to the kids about the plan.

TyAnn told Mom, "Oh, please don't leave me behind with him. He's a monster and will force me to work night and day doing all his chores."

Mom looked at TyAnn like she had gone bonkers. "I thought you liked your brother?"

"Oh I do," TyAnn replied. "I just want to let him know up front that I will not do his chores for him."

"I don't think he will expect you to do his chores," Mom said.

"Oh, Mom, I'm only kidding. You know Bubby and I will get along fine, and you don't have to worry about us. Besides Grandma and Grandpa are only a call away, if we need anything," TyAnn reassured Mom.

"I've never been out west," Mom said and then sighed.

"You should go and have a nice vacation—just you and Daddy."

TyAnn convinced Mom. Dad made the necessary

arrangements, and they flew off to Denver. They were to be gone for three weeks. They decided to spend the extra week by themselves on a second honeymoon.

Back at home, TyAnn took charge of the kitchen. She made Robert his favorite meal, just like Mom did—cheeseburgers and fries. Grandma helped and made meals for them and had Robert come out and pick up the food. Sunday afternoon TyAnn and Robert visited Grandma and Grandpa, like normal. The first week went smoothly and the kids got along great. Robert was in charge of the money, and he had to pay some of the bills while Mom and Dad were away. He felt very grownup as he took care of the house and his sister.

One night a violent thunderstorm woke Robert out of a sound sleep. He heard a loud clap of thunder and a bolt of lightning seemed to come from right outside his room. Lightning had hit one of the trees in the front yard, and a large branch fell to the ground. Robert raced into TyAnn's room to check on her. He found her sitting up in bed shaking like a leaf. Charger sat on her haunches next to her bed. Robert sat beside her and put his arm around her shoulder.

"Everything will be okay, Tanny," he said in a reassuring voice to comfort her.

She didn't have to say anything. Robert knew she was frightened. She finally managed to say, "Bubby, I really don't like storms," in a childlike whisper.

The storm lasted for an hour and Robert stayed in her room to keep her company. After the storm was over, Robert asked, "Will you be all right by yourself, Tanny?"

She meekly answered, "I will be okay as long as Charger stays with me."

Robert looked at Charger and laughed. Charger cocked her head to the side as if trying to listen better to her instructions. "Charger, you stay here with Tanny and protect her, okay?"

Charger wagged her tail and barked once as if to answer in the affirmative. Robert went back to his room and fell asleep.

Mom called early the next morning. TyAnn answered the

phone and told Mom about the storm. "The maple tree in the front by the sidewalk lost a big branch, and there were leaves and small branches all over the yard. Bubby is moving the big limb out of the way, so we can get the car out of the driveway."

"Were you afraid?" Mom asked.

"I was a little scared."

Mom knew that she was probably more than a little frightened, but didn't say anything more.

"We will be home in ten days, sweetie," Mom said.

Robert came back in the house. He needed TyAnn's help to move the big branch a bit more. She quickly threw on a t-shirt and shorts and headed out to help Robert. She stood behind him as they tugged on the limb to move it out of the way. Robert slipped on the wet grass, and they both fell down. Robert landed on top of her and got up with a funny look on his face. TyAnn looked at Robert. "What's wrong? Why are you staring at me?"

Robert didn't say anything at first, so TyAnn asked again, "What's wrong, Bubby?"

Robert blushed as he told her, "You've got breasts."

"I'm not a baby anymore. I even wear bras!" she said just to embarrass him more. She reached out her hand and said, "Help me up."

"Did I hurt you when I fell on you?" Robert asked.

"I'm okay," TyAnn replied, as she rubbed her chest where Robert had fallen hard on her.

"I'm sorry, Tanny. I slipped," Robert told her gently. "We can wait until later to move this branch. I can get the car around it if I need to go somewhere."

They walked back toward the house together.

"Mom called to see if we were all right. She asked me if I was afraid last night, and I told a little white lie. I told her I was just scared a little, but I was scared a lot. I don't know what I would have done if you weren't here."

Robert put his hand on her back and told her, "We will always be there for each other, even when we get old and you are all wrinkled up like a prune."

TyAnn turned to him and elbowed him in the ribs. "Prune, huh?" She elbowed him again for good measure. "That's for falling on my breast," she teased him as she scampered back to the house.

In the afternoon Laurie Roland and her father stopped by the house to make sure they were all right. Laurie's father helped Robert pull the branch out of the way. He offered to come back later with his chainsaw and cut it up if he could have it for firewood. Robert told him he could have all the wood.

Mom and Dad returned from their trip, and Robert and TyAnn picked them up at the airport in St. Louis. Mom listened patiently as TyAnn caught Mom up on everything that happened while they were gone.

Robert told Mom, "Tanny has learned to cook pretty good. She is getting better at boiling water. She only burned the toast a few times, and her cheeseburgers don't taste like charcoal anymore."

TyAnn punched him in the side.

"You don't look like you have been starving," Mom replied.

"Can we have fried chicken and mashed potatoes for supper tonight?" Robert pleaded.

"I will make it," TyAnn said hopefully.

Robert groaned in the backseat.

Chapter Twenty-Two

Robert and TyAnn spent the last two weeks of July and the first two weeks of August at the farm helping Grandma and Grandpa again. Grandpa had been in the hospital, so much of the heavy work fell on the shoulders of Robert, David and Chuck. Grandpa would supervise the work, but couldn't do much. Not being able to work as he always had frustrated Grandpa. TyAnn would help Grandma prepare the meals. One night TyAnn made the entire supper by herself.

"We won't tell Grandpa or Robert and see what they have to say," Grandma suggested.

"That will be a good surprise. Will you watch me cook, but don't say anything, unless I do something really wrong."

Later, Grandpa and Robert stuffed themselves at the table.

"Thanks, Grandma! Everything was delicious," Robert complimented her.

"Are you sure it was all right? The chicken wasn't too dry, or the potatoes too lumpy? How was the gravy?"

Robert said, "Everything was perfect. Nobody can cook like you, Grandma."

Grandma smiled at TyAnn. "Don't thank me for supper because your little sister cooked it all by herself. I stood by and watched, and didn't have to say a thing to her."

"No! Really?" Robert looked at TyAnn. He wasn't sure he could believe what Grandma had said.

Two hours later, TyAnn caught Robert looking in the refrigerator for some more chicken. "What are you looking for, Robert?" she asked sternly.

"Nothing," he answered. "In fact, I'm feeling sick to my stomach. I think you poisoned me."

"If you want some more of MY fried chicken, you simply have to ask. I might let you have more, if Grandpa doesn't want it," TyAnn said with a trace of pride in her voice.

"Okay, Tanny, your chicken tasted as good as Grandma's. All right. Does that make you happy? I liked your cooking. There, I admit it."

TyAnn smiled as she walked away. "You can have one more piece, but that's all."

76

TyAnn and Robert helped Grandma in the garden and worked very hard for an entire week—helping with canning and preserving. Grandma told them to take Friday off and have fun. TyAnn wanted to go swimming and didn't want to go by herself. Robert was reluctant but agreed to go along. They headed down to the pond.

Robert asked TyAnn, "Where is your bathing suit?"

"I'm not going to wear one."

Robert stopped and told her, "No way. You are not going skinny dipping. Not happening."

TyAnn looked at him and said, "What do you think I was doing two days ago when Laurie and I went down to the pond while you were playing ball with David and Chuck and Kevin?"

Robert looked at her and shook his head. He knew something but didn't tell TyAnn. "You know you aren't supposed to go swimming by yourself, TyAnn Allyson Benjamin. If Dad knew that, he would paddle your butt, no matter how old you are."

"I wasn't by myself! Laurie was with me."

"You know that Dad wants me, or David, around if you want to go swimming."

"Are you going to tell Daddy?"

"Not this time, if you promise never to do it again."

"All right! I promise. I won't go swimming in the pond unless you or David are around. Does that mean I should ask David to go skinny dipping with me?"

"If you want him to see you naked, go right ahead."

"You know I won't do that. I'm gonna wear my underwear to go swimming. It's dark blue and no one can see anything."

They continued to the pond and Robert stripped down to his shorts and jumped in from the bank. TyAnn took off her top and shorts and gingerly walked into the pond. The water felt so good. The temperature had been in the high 90s for over a week. Grandma's and Grandpa's house was not air conditioned, and it had been hard to sleep at night with the heat. TyAnn splashed Robert and he dunked her under the water. They had fun relaxing and playing, just like when they were kids, and they soon forgot the time. Robert thought he heard Grandma calling.

"TyAnn, be quiet. Is that Grandma calling?"

She listened for a moment. "I can hear her now."

Sure enough, Grandma was calling them to dinner. Robert figured it must be about noon, as he looked at the sun overhead.

"Come on, Tanny. Grandma is calling. We don't want to keep her waiting."

Robert climbed out of the pond and got his shirt, shoes and socks on in a hurry. TyAnn took longer to get dressed.

"Wait for me, Bubby," she called as Robert started to head back. Robert waited as she hurried to catch up. They got back and Grandma had some dinner for them.

"I was starting to worry about you kids. I almost sent Grandpa out to look for you. Now eat your lunch and have some lemonade. It is too hot to work this afternoon."

They ate outside on the back porch because they were still soaking wet. The sun felt good as they ate a sandwich and a piece of pecan pie. Grandma had cool lemonade for them to drink. They had the afternoon to do whatever they wanted.

TyAnn suggested, "Let's walk over to see David."

"That's fine with me."

TyAnn went in the house to change clothes so she didn't smell so much like the pond. They hiked over to Uncle Charlie's to find David—it was only half a mile away.

"Hey, guys. What brings you out on such a hot afternoon?" David asked.

"Grandma gave us the day off, so we were looking for something to do. Do you have chores to do?" Robert asked.

"I'm all finished."

"What do you wanna do?"

"Let's walk into Almaville to get some candy bars, drink some pop and play pinball like we used to when we were kids. Oh, I guess you are still a kid, TyAnn," David teased her.

She stuck out her tongue then said, "I want to buy six candy bars because they only cost a quarter."

It was about two miles to the little crossroad hamlet, which had a gas station and a small store with a pinball machine. They talked as they plodded slowly along the hilly narrow road into town.

"Has Grandma been keeping you guys busy this week?"

"You better believe it! We have been canning and preserving all kinds of stuff."

"Robert even had to do the chores that Grandpa had trouble with. He's usually in bed asleep by nine o'clock."

"It's been so hot, too."

"Grandma told us it was too hot to work today, so we went swimming," Robert told David.

TyAnn looked at Robert, then told David, "I went skinny dipping!"

"What!? You didn't really, did you?"

"No, I wore my underwear. Nobody could see me except Bubby, and he doesn't count. Laurie and I went swimming while you guys were playing ball the other day."

"Swimming or..."

"Skinny dipping! Both of us," TyAnn said as she grinned.

"We almost quit playing ball so we could go swimming. If we had, we would had seen you two," David mentioned, as he picked up a rock and threw it at a telephone pole. He nailed the pole from sixty feet away.

Robert looked at TyAnn. She blushed as she thought about what might have happened.

In the summer one of the local farmers operated a fruit stand along the highway through Almaville. That day he had sweet corn, a few watermelons and some fresh peaches.

"Peaches sound better than candy bars," Robert suggested.

"Absolutely. Fresh peaches win," David agreed.

"Yeah, because peaches don't melt like chocolate does," TyAnn answered with a bit of sarcasm.

They had enough money to buy two peaches apiece and had enough leftover for pop and a few games of pinball. TyAnn noticed an old tire swing next to the farmstand and wanted to use it. She swung as Robert and David watched. They had fun, then headed back to David's house. Along the way TyAnn stepped in a hole on the side of the road and turned her ankle. She had trouble walking so Robert carried her piggyback-style. After awhile he complained, "You are getting too big to carry."

"You mean you are not as strong as you thought," TyAnn teased.

Robert set her down. "Just for that crack, you can walk the rest of the way."

She tried but her ankle hurt too much. Robert and David were walking away and she had to yell at them. "Bubby, I'm sorry. Don't leave me here."

Robert stopped and turned around. He shrugged his shoulders in resignation at the thought of carrying her all the way back.

David offered, "I'll carry her for awhile. She can't be that heavy."

She climbed up on his back and he asked her, "TyAnn, how much do you weigh?"

"That's not a polite thing to ask a lady," she said as she tipped his baseball cap forward until it covered his eyes.

"I'm not asking a lady. I'm asking you," David teased.

She smacked him and said, "Almost eighty pounds if you must know."

"Feels more like a hundred and eighty!"

David carried her most of the way home, then Robert took over. By the time they reached David's house, her ankle was feeling better. She jumped down off Robert's back and sprinted to the house.

"Thanks for the ride. My ankle feels better now."

"You stinker! You're gonna get it," Robert yelled at her and took off after her. He caught her just before she got to the door. He grabbed her and threw her over his shoulder. He carried her to the muddy area out behind the old wash house. Years ago the area was a small pond that supplied water for doing the laundry. Now it was merely a muddy depression with only a bit of water in the bottom. "Should we throw her in the mudhole for making us carry her back?" Robert asked.

David replied, "I don't know if we should. It's pretty deep. Last week a cow got stuck in there, and all I could see was the top of the cow. The rest of the cow was stuck deep in the mud. We had to get a tractor to pull her out."

TyAnn squirmed as Robert stiffened his hold on her.

"I think we should throw her in," Robert decided.

"Okay, she's your sister! We might had to hose her off afterward. That is, if we can even find her later," David answered back.

David followed, laughing as TyAnn struggled for a

moment, then went totally limp. She pretended to have fainted, but Robert knew better. He tickled her side, and she couldn't help but giggle. They grabbed TyAnn, with each of them holding an arm and a leg. They swung her back and forth—higher and higher. She was silent until she screamed, "Bubby!" at the top of her lungs. Robert couldn't hold his laughter in anymore. They set her down on the grass and fell down beside her. She laid down on the grass and laughed with them.

"Pulling a cow out with a tractor. That's good. How long did it take you bozos to think of that?" she teased.

At that moment Uncle Charlie came around the corner. "Hey, you kids shouldn't be playing so close to that mudhole. I nearly lost a cow in there last week," he declared to TyAnn as he winked at Robert.

TyAnn looked at Uncle Charlie, then the mudhole. She wasn't sure if he was kidding or not and backed up a few feet. The boys laughed because they knew Uncle Charlie was teasing her.

Chapter Twenty-Three

"Why does summer seem to go so fast, and the school year takes forever?" TyAnn complained to Robert as they sat outside on the front porch drinking Dr Pepper.

"Maybe because the school year is three times as long as summer vacation."

"I know that! I was speaking rhetorically."

"You learned a new word over the summer, huh?" Robert teased TyAnn.

School started before they were mentally prepared to go back. Regardless, within a few days they were back in the swing of things. Robert was elected president of his senior class.

TyAnn asked, "How many times did you vote for yourself. I heard there were 127 ballots cast. Not bad for a class of thirty-five kids!"

TyAnn was elected vice-president of her freshman class. She signed up for all the after school clubs she could squeeze into her busy schedule. Dad was the math teacher for the high school, and Robert had had him for math every year. Now TyAnn had him as a teacher, also. She felt funny having to call him "Mr. Benjamin" in class and accidentally called him "Daddy" several times. The other students laughed and eventually Dad gave up and let her call him Dad in class.

"You are spoiled rotten, Tanny. I never got away with that. I still can't."

TyAnn teased Robert by saying, "Just proves that Daddy loves me more."

Mom still taught second grade and used the family car to get to work. The rest of the family walked to school, except during inclement weather, then TyAnn complained.

Robert said, "You won't melt!"

"But my hair will get all messed up."

"You have your hair in a ponytail!"

She batted her eyes and got a ride in Dad's old Ford.

The senior class traditionally put on a play in the fall. This year most seniors assumed another Tennessee Hummingway play would be the obvious choice, but at the last minute, they changed

82

their minds and chose a new comedy by the relatively unknown author, Max McGee, entitled *Forever... A Love Story*. Robert had a good part, but was not the lead character this year. Laurie Roland had the female lead again with Kevin Ambuehl cast as her boyfriend. Good casting since they were going steady anyway. One week before the play was supposed to be presented, the student who played the "girlfriend" of Robert's character came down with the measles and had to be replaced. Having no other seniors available to take the part left Mrs. Sheffield, the play's director, in a quandary. Robert was eating supper the day after, and mentioned it to Dad.

"Mrs. Sheffield doesn't know who to get to fill in as understudy. She's really desperate."

TyAnn had been helping Robert with his lines, and knew most of the play by heart already. She knew someone who could step in and take over the small part.

TyAnn announced at supper, "I know the perfect person to take over for Louisa."

"Who?" Robert asked. He took the bait.

TyAnn batted her eyes and flipped her ponytail around. Before she could say another word, Robert jumped in, "Oh, no! No way, not in this lifetime!"

"Why not?" TyAnn asked. "How many senior girls are not already involved in the play, in one capacity or another?"

"Well, all of them have some part in production or stage roles or something."

Robert realized he didn't have a chance of winning this argument.

The next day at school, TyAnn approached Mrs. Sheffield, and boldly announced that not only could she play the part of "Missy Calhoun," but she already knew all the lines. Mrs. Sheffield listened to an impromptu audition and agreed to give TyAnn a shot. At practice that evening TyAnn knew all the lines perfectly, and even got laughs at all the right times. She had the whole group laughing when, at one point, her character had to jump in Robert's arms when she was frightened by a loud noise. Robert realized that she was actually better suited for the part than Louisa.

83

The play was performed on Friday and Saturday nights and both nights the gym was packed. The play was an even bigger success than last year's more well-known play. During the performance Friday, TyAnn improvised a little and kissed Robert on the cheek after she jumped in his arms. She repeated the kiss on Saturday because the audience loved it. TyAnn got a dozen roses from Dad after Saturday night's performance and something even better from Robert. He told her that she was the best part of the play, and kissed her on the cheek.

Chapter Twenty-Four

"Finally, basketball season has arrived," Robert shouted as he grabbed a ball from the rack and took a shot. It clanged off the front of the rim.

"Hey! I thought you've been practicing," Coach Anderson hollered.

"I have been, Coach. Really, I have."

Practice started with the whole team ready to kick some butt. More specifically, Mount Trenton's butt. Coach Anderson whipped the boys into the best shape of their lives. They ran and ran and ran at practice, then ran even more. With everybody who played on the varsity last year returning, and some juniors and sophomores with talent, they were deeper than any other Kinmundy Junction team had ever been. Of course it also paid to have two players the quality of Robert Benjamin and David Tomanek on the team. Coach Anderson expected them to be good, but even he was pleasantly surprised when they beat Palmerton by forty-eight points in their first game. Coach Anderson had them press full court for the entire game. Using different types of pressure, the Hornets kept the Wooden Shoes on their heels and confused the whole game. Before the holidays no team came within thirty points of the Hornets, who were playing with an intensity and confidence that none of the townspeople had ever seen. They had something to prove and were working hard to accomplish their goal. Robert had only one goal for the year—to win the state championship. Not even beating Mount Trenton would satisfy him.

At Christmas-time Coach Anderson had a surprise for them. They had been invited to play in the prestigious Little Egypt Holiday Tournament in Carbondale. The tournament was one of the oldest in the state and annually boasted sixteen top teams. Adler-Trout Gym, on the campus of SIU, hosted the games. This gave Robert even more motivation since that was where he would play his college ball, along with David. Coach Anderson knew he had taken a big chance with the team because a couple losses in the tournament could have a negative effect on their confidence. He needn't had been worried. Kinmundy Junction surprised the entire state by winning the tournament easily. No team came closer than twenty-two points to them. After winning the tournament, someone started voting for the Hornets in the state rankings. Every week for the rest of the year Kinmundy Junction received at least one vote in the poll. Coach Anderson constantly worried about the biggest obstacle in his team's path to the championship. Mount Trenton sat atop the polls as the number one ranked team in the state. They had their best team in years with the addition of two new players from Missouri, the Hilton twins. Coach Anderson knew that this year it would be even harder to beat them.

In early January Kinmundy Junction had their two easiest games of the year. At least they should have been, according to most fans. On Tuesday, January 5, the Hornets traveled through falling snow to Patoka City, which had only won one game all year. The Hornets took it easy, yet still won by fifty-seven points. Coach rested the starters for part of the first half and all of the last quarter. Even the partisan Patoka City fans were impressed at how good the Hornets were playing this year. Coach Anderson apologized to the Patoka City coach after the game.

"I'm sorry about the score, Jess."

"Bill, you don't have to apologize. You did everything you could, short of using eighth graders. My kids are not in the same class as your team. This could be the year you guys get past Mount Trenton. Good luck the rest of the way. I'm glad we don't have to play you guys anymore this year."

On Friday the Hornets would host their arch rivals from LaGrove, who had only won three games. The won-and-lost records didn't matter when these schools faced each other; the games were always hard fought contests.

Chapter Twenty-Five

On Wednesday afternoon as Mom and TyAnn drove home from Millstown, the rain that had been falling, turned to ice. It soon coated the highway in a thin sheet making travel perilous. Mom slowed down coming around the curve by the park at the edge of town.

"Hang on, TyAnn. I think that truck is going too fast!" Mom hollered.

Mom's statement proved to be prophetic. The oncoming truck lost control and collided with them, sending the car spinning in circles until it came to an abrupt stop as it hit a tree. The driver of the truck managed to get his truck stopped and hurried over to help. Mom was hurt and bleeding, but TyAnn was in worse condition. Another car came along and stopped. The driver raced to a nearby house, and they called for an ambulance. The ambulance arrived momentarily and took Mom and TyAnn to the Millstown hospital. Mom was treated for cuts and bruises, but was not seriously injured. TyAnn had not fared as well. She was in critical condition. Coach Anderson's sister, a nurse at the hospital, happened to be on duty. She knew Mom and TyAnn. She called the school trying to get in touch with Coach Anderson. The school secretary took the call. She hurried to the gym to get the coach. He told the boys to scrimmage until he got back.

He took the call.

"Bill, there's been an accident involving Emma Benjamin and TyAnn. Emma is going to be all right, but TyAnn is in serious condition. I thought I should let you know since Robert is probably at practice with you."

"Thanks for calling, sis. Do you have any idea how it happened or anything? Does Jim know?"

"A truck lost control and hit their car. That's all I know so far. I called the house, but the phone was busy, so I don't know if Jim knows about the accident or not."

"I'll take care of telling the boys, and see if I can track down Jim."

Coach said a quick prayer as he headed back to the gym. He immediately stopped practice and pulled Robert, David and Chuck over to the side.

"Robert, your Mom and TyAnn have been in an accident. Your Mom is all right, but TyAnn is hurt. We need to get you home and find your Dad. I'm not sure if he knows about the accident yet."

The three boys sprinted to the Benjamin home, still in their practice gear, and found Dad who had been on the phone with the police.

"Dad, do you know what happened? Are they all right?" Robert asked.

"All I know is that the accident was caused by ice on the road. We need to get to the hospital."

Dad was obviously upset and didn't say anymore. Coach Anderson arrived a minute later. Coach looked at Jim and could tell the news was not good. Dad, Robert, David and Chuck got into the old Ford and headed to Millstown. The rain that had turned into ice and caused the accident had stopped. The road remained wet, but not icy, as they carefully made their way to the Millstown hospital. They met Mom in the emergency room, but TyAnn was upstairs in the intensive care unit. TyAnn remained unconscious, and the doctors had to run tests. Mom, Dad and the boys were forced to wait in a lounge and weren't allowed to see TyAnn yet. Soon Uncle Charlie arrived, stayed for an hour, then took David and Chuck home. Mom, Dad and Robert spent the night at the hospital. They waited all through the evening for any word of how TyAnn was doing. The doctors worked as fast and carefully as they could to keep her stable. Finally, after six hours of waiting, a doctor came out to talk to Mom and Dad. For ten minutes the doctor explained to them what had happened and what to expect. The news was not good. Dad came back to talk to Robert as Mom was allowed to see TyAnn briefly. TyAnn was unresponsive, but Mom held her hand and talked to her, anyway. When the time came for her to leave, Mom kissed TyAnn on the forehead and whispered in her ear, "I love you, baby."

Robert went back home after his parents insisted, so he could go to school. Mom and Dad stayed at the hospital all day Thursday and overnight into Friday morning. Coach Anderson canceled Thursday's basketball practice. Robert went back to the hospital as soon as school let out. Mom and Dad drove home to change clothes, get a bit of rest, and something to eat. They came back later so Robert could go home to sleep.

The school tried to cancel Friday's game, but LaGrove would not agree to a cancellation and make-up game. Robert stayed in school part of Friday, then got a ride to the hospital from Uncle Charlie. There had been no change in TyAnn's condition and the doctors were thinking about having her moved to Childrens Memorial in St. Louis. Robert stayed until six o'clock, when he had leave to get back for the game.

That night Robert's mind, and that of the whole team, was anywhere but on a basketball game. They were totally unfocused, and most of the crowd knew why. Soon the whole crowd knew about the accident, and LaGrove's refusal to reschedule the game. There had always been an intense rivalry between the two towns, and tonight would fuel an even greater animosity. The junior varsity game was marred by a shoving match between two of the players. Coach Anderson sent Steve Doudera to the locker room to shower and cool off. The Hornets JV team won by seven points, but the game was physical, and the two referees had a difficult time keeping tempers at bay.

The varsity game followed, and the boys played like their feet were encased in cement. They missed easy shots, made mental mistakes and were not communicating on defense. Coach called a timeout and tried to inject some energy into the boys. In other words, he yelled at them.

"You are not talking to each other. You have to call out screens. Roger, you are letting that skinny center get position wherever he wants. Make him work. Use your size and strength. Stop letting him push you around. Chuck, if you can't move your feet on defense, you are going to sit on the bench."

No one was spared as Coach lit into every one of them. Not even Robert escaped a tongue lashing. Coach sent them back on the court, but nothing changed. He didn't know what to do. He sent in the second string, but they were not in any better mood to play. At the half the score was 30-10 against the home team. The team slumped on the bench in the locker room. Coach Anderson remained outside. Shortly before the team had to return to the floor, Mr. Benjamin entered the locker room. Robert didn't know what to think and imagined the worst had happened. He started to cry as Dad sat next to him. Dad placed an arm around Robert's shoulders to comfort his son and said, "TyAnn's condition has not changed. She is still unconscious, but her vital signs are stable. That is good news at least."

Robert nodded.

Dad told the team, "I appreciate your concern for TyAnn, but you need to concentrate on the game for the next two quarters. When TyAnn wakes up, I don't want to have to tell her that the Hornets lost to LaGrove on their home court. You haven't lost a home game in four years, and you had better not start tonight!"

Though still saddened by the accident, the Hornets managed to concentrate their focus and energy for the second half. LaGrove didn't stand a chance. The boys rallied and held LaGrove to fifteen points in the second half and managed to win by a score of 65-45. It was their closest game of the year so far, but one of their most satisfying victories. After the game Robert returned to the hospital and stayed overnight. Mom and Dad returned home to get some sleep.

In the morning, the nurse gave Robert permission to see TyAnn for a moment. He squeezed her hand as he talked to her. He didn't know if she could hear him or not, but then she squeezed his hand back. He looked at her bruised and bandaged face, and she opened her eyes and saw him.

"Bubby, where am I?"

She managed to ask before falling asleep. Mom and Dad rushed back to the hospital, and three hours later TyAnn woke up again. She saw Mom and Dad with Robert. "I'm thirsty. Can I have some water?"

Mom helped TyAnn sip a little bit of water. She looked at the clock and asked, "What day is it?"

"Saturday morning, baby," Mom replied. "You've been in the hospital since Wednesday afternoon."

TyAnn looked at Bubby and asked, "How bad did you beat LaGrove?"

Robert laughed through his tears. "We beat them by twenty."

"Is that all? You should have beat them by fifty."

They knew she was going to be all right.

Chapter Twenty-Six

TyAnn came home from the hospital Tuesday afternoon after spending a week there. She returned to school the next morning. All of her classmates wanted to sign the cast on her left arm. She made sure the basketball team signed the cast first though.

One night before she went to sleep, Robert came in her room to talk to her. She had heard about the LaGrove game and how poorly they had played in the first half. Robert sat on the side of her bed with her.

"Coach didn't even come into the locker room. The whole team just sat there and no one said a word. When Dad came into the locker room, I thought he was going to tell me you were gone."

"You mean gone like dead gone?" TyAnn asked.

Robert nodded.

"Oh, Bubby, that must had been so scary."

"It was the worst moment of my life, Tanny," Robert said. "What would I do without you."

TyAnn put her arm around him as Robert softly cried. She didn't even tease him. Within two weeks she had returned to normal, except for the cast, which she used to club Robert everyday.

The rest of the regular season was anticlimactic. The close call against LaGrove had refocused the team. The Hornets won the rest of their games, and no team came within twenty-five points. The blowouts allowed Coach Anderson to give the bench plenty of playing time. He knew the game experience would benefit them the following year. They won the conference tournament and went into the regional with intense determination. The first two games were blowouts. The Hornets won by thirty-eight and forty-three points. Mount Trenton also won easily, though. The Wildcats had lost only one game all year. Friday night the gym was packed with the largest crowd ever to witness a game in Mount Trenton. The place was louder than ever. Coach Anderson noticed the referees were not the same ones as last year. Mount Trenton won the tip and set up their half-court offense. Robert anticipated a pass to one of the Hilton twins, made a steal and drove in for a layup. He dunked the ball with two hands, and the Hornets never looked back. Mount Trenton was down by fifteen at the half, and the Hornets ended up winning by twenty-six points. The memory of the bad call that ended the game the previous year had been obliterated. Robert was jubilant as he celebrated with his teammates. He saw TyAnn, picked her up, hugged her, then swung her around in a circle. Coach Anderson walked over to shake hands with Jim Wasem, the Mount Trenton coach of many years.

"Congratulations, Bill. You deserve the victory. Your team played better tonight."

"We had a group of very determined players this year. I think they might be the team to win it all."

"Before tonight, I thought the same about my team. I figured we were going to win our third state title this year, but we came up against a better team tonight. I wish you luck the rest of the way. Maybe now the rest of the state will learn that the kids from Kinmundy Junction can play ball."

In the locker room after the game, as the kids whooped and hollered, Coach sat quietly on a folding chair for a couple minutes. He felt the weight of the world had been lifted from his shoulders. Maybe now Kinmundy Junction would be taken seriously. He stood up and got their attention. "I want to tell you boys how proud I am of you regardless of what happens from here on out."

Robert said, "Coach, we just beat the top-ranked team in the state on their home floor. We have seven more games to win, and we plan on doing just that."

The sectional round of the tournament was easier than the regional. The Hornets easily beat their opponents by an average of twenty-seven points a game. The only scary moment happened in the Wednesday game when Chuck twisted an ankle. He sat the rest of that game and was not needed in the sectional championship on Friday night.

By Tuesday, the night of the supersectional, Chuck was ready to go. Tuesday night the Hornets traveled to West Charleston to face the Gothenburg City Flaming Hearts. The Hearts had a lineup of giants. They had two players who were six-ten and another player six-eight.

During the warm-ups Robert and David watched their

opponents. Robert nudged David and said, "Watch number 55."

"Yeah, he's pretty tall," David replied.

"Every time he dips his shoulder to go up for a shot he brings the ball down to his chest."

David watched then smiled.

"He becomes just another player," Robert said.

"Are you thinking what I'm thinking?" David asked.

Robert grinned as he nodded.

The Hornets were not impressed after Robert blocked the first shot attempted by the Flaming Hearts center. The Hornets had too much speed and quickness and overwhelmed the slower taller players. The final score was closer than the actual game, as Coach Anderson played his second string the last five minutes. Still, the Hornets won 84-59.

Chapter Twenty-Seven

The Hornets Are Going To State! The local paper put out a special edition with that headline. The whole town closed up on Friday as the Hornets and their fans headed to the Assembly Hall in Champaign. The Hornets would play in the opening game Friday afternoon against the Thornton Central Wildcats. Once the game got underway, it seemed that all of the fans, who were not from Thornton, were rooting for the Cinderella team from Kinmundy Junction. Many of the same fans had been here the previous year when Covington made a run at the title.

The first half was close with the lead changing hands eight times. The Hornets trailed by one point at the half. Coach Anderson changed strategy at the half. To open the second half, the Hornets were in a zone defense designed to stop the Wildcats center from getting the ball in the lane. The strategy worked, and the Wildcats become frustrated and turned the ball over twenty-one times in the second half alone. The Hornets won going away by twenty-three points. They were guaranteed a trophy.

Robert told the team, "We are not settling for just a trophy. There is only one trophy that we want."

The rest of the team agreed with Robert.

Friday night at the motel, Coach Anderson told the team a story about three other small schools.

"Back in 1952 there was a team from Hebron. That's way up north almost in Wisconsin. They were even smaller than our school, I think. Anyway, they played against the same school we will face tomorrow. In Indiana there was a team from a small town, Milan, and they beat Muncie Central, one of the biggest schools in the state to win the championship. Just last year we watched on this very court as the Covington Cornhuskers almost won the title."

The boys remembered that game well. Coach Anderson asked them, "Do we want to be Cornhuskers? Do we want to be Cornhuskers?" he repeated for emphasis.

"No!" the whole team shouted as one voice. "We are Hornets, and we play like champions!"

"Get some rest boys. Tomorrow we play two games."

Before the team left the motel Saturday for the Assembly Hall, they gathered for breakfast.

TyAnn sat by Robert and casually mentioned, "I know you have been a little preoccupied with basketball the last couple days, but you have forgotten something very important. Do you remember what today's date is?"

Robert thought for a moment. It suddenly dawned on him.

TyAnn laughed as she told him, "Happy birthday, doofus."

Saturday afternoon—Assembly Hall. The Hornets took the court for their pre-game warm-up and were kept loose by the humor of Kevin Ambuehl. Coach Anderson brought them over to the bench for some final instructions.

"Have any of you boys been on TV before this weekend?"

Of course none of them had. "When I was a kid, I used to go the the movies all the time. I used to watch these western serials that were popular at the time. Every Saturday morning there would be a new episode. There was usually a sidekick to the main star. The sidekick was always the funny one it seemed." Coach chuckled as he looked at Kevin.

The boys were wondering why Coach was telling them this right now.

"Anyway, I was thinking about those old movies."

Robert spoke up, "Coach, are you going to tell us what to do about the game?"

"Oh, yeah. I forgot about the game. Well, I suppose you guys know what to do by now. You've been playing as a team for four years now. I remember that first practice when you were freshmen. I had to scrimmage against the seniors, who were bigger and more experienced. You kids played as a team and whooped them." He paused for a moment and closed his eyes. When he opened them, he said, "Y'all go out there and have some fun. I'm going to sit back and enjoy the game while you kick their butts. I might even get in my afternoon nap. If I do fall asleep, don't you guys wake me up, or else I'll make you run extra laps!" Coach laughed and soon the whole team was cracking up on the bench.

When the game started, Quincy Falls, a long-time basketball powerhouse, had trouble settling down. They turned the ball over repeatedly and the Hornets took advantage. At halftime the Hornets led by twelve points. Robert caught fire as the second half started and made six shots in a row to double the lead. Quincy Falls never recovered and the Hornets won by twenty-three. The boys showered and came back out to watch the second game.

"They aren't even tired," Coach Anderson told Jim Benjamin.

"They're so used to playing ball all day that a thirty-two minute game is barely enough to work up a sweat."

Dad watched the second game between Collinsville and Lockport with Coach Anderson. He picked up on something that Lockport did that he thought the Hornets could exploit. In the third quarter of the game, it became obvious who the Hornets opponent would be. The boys headed back to the motel for some food and rest.

On the bus ride back to the Assembly Hall later that evening, Robert sat with TyAnn.

"Do you think it will be close?" she asked.

"Nah, we will beat them by thirty points," Robert joked.

"Really," TyAnn answered sarcastically.

Robert asked TyAnn, "Do you remember the homemade basket Dad made for us when we were little kids?"

"Of course I remember it. It's still in the storage shed, you know."

"Remember how I used to make you count backward from five down to zero as I was shooting?"

TyAnn nodded.

"That was preparation for today. Today I am going to make the winning basket as the clock runs out."

Collinsville beat Quincy Falls to claim third place before the Hornets took the court. Before the game Dad had a chance to talk one last time with Uncle Bill, or rather Coach Anderson. Coach Anderson thought Dad's suggestion would work. The Lockport squad relied too much on their star player, Danny Chase. Coach wanted to make Chase work extra hard on the defensive end to wear him out. When the Hornets were on defense they planned to triple team Chase and make him give up the ball. If the other players could make shots, it would be a good game, but Coach didn't think the supporting cast from Lockport was up to the challenge.

The Hornets won the tip and moved into their offensive set. Robert called for play number five and the Hornets scored on a backdoor cut. They hurried back on defense and didn't pressure the Spartans. That alone surprised the Lockport coach who had been expecting full court pressure all game long. The Hornets set up their defense to stop Chase. Roger used his strength to push Chase farther out on the court than he wanted. Roger continually denied Chase his favorite spot. Robert and David guarded Chase from the front to deny easy passing lanes. Lockport held the ball for two minutes as they tried to work it in to their star player. A Spartan guard made an ill-advised pass into the lane and David intercepted. He passed the ball up-court to Robert and the Hornet fast break worked to perfection. Kevin Ambuehl scored on a layup and the rout was on. At the end of the first quarter, the Hornets were up by eight. They stretched the lead to fifteen by halftime. The Hornets grabbed every rebound and ran their fast break for easy transition baskets.

Lockport was confused by the Hornets defense. One time they would fall back into a zone and the next time they might apply full-court pressure. Coach Anderson never seemed to have to tell them what defense to use. Lockport's Coach Bob Parzych couldn't figure out how the Hornets were changing their defense so quickly. He watched Coach Anderson trying to figure it out, but gave up because Coach Anderson didn't even talk to his team. He sat on his chair and seemed to be bored. Coach Parzych thought, "How can he be so calm. He looks like he's reading a newspaper at the barber shop waiting to get a haircut."

In the locker room at halftime Coach Anderson told his team, "They are so confused on offense. They are tentative because they don't know what defense they will face every time up the court. Robert, it will be more difficult this half to see me. Do you want to call the defenses yourself?"

"Let's try it, and if I screw up, then we will change back."

What the Lockport coach, or any other coach they had faced, didn't know was that Coach Anderson had worked out a set of silent signals for the defense. Most of the time the Hornets used a stifling man-to-man defense, but on occasions, they would switch to a zone. Coach used his position on the chair, or the bench depending on the gym, to signal Robert. Back home in their small gym, it was easy to see him along the sidelines. The size of the Assembly Hall made that more difficult.

Robert started calling the defense in the second half. Most of the time they stayed in the zone that kept it difficult for Lockport to get the ball inside. They would settle for outside shots. If the shot missed, the Hornets would grab the rebound and run. They pushed the ball up court for easy baskets. The Spartans didn't give up though and cut the lead to nine points in the third quarter. Coach called a timeout to settle the boys down.

"Is anyone tired? If not then we were going to our zone press for the rest of the quarter. Make it look like man to man pressure at first, then drop into zone pressure. Everyone know your assignments? All right, let's go!"

They scored again when Robert hit a jumper from the free throw line. The Spartans were finished. The third quarter ended with the Hornets up by twenty-two. The Hornets kept the pressure on and built the lead to twenty-nine with two minutes left in the game. Coach began substituting at that point. He removed the starters from the game, one at a time. David was removed with a minute to go and Robert came out of the game fifteen seconds later. The final score was 79-50. Robert saw TyAnn after the game was over, and she pointed to the scoreboard.

"You promised me we were going to win by thirty."

"Sorry, Tanny," Robert said as she jumped into his arms and he twirled her around.

"At least you made the winning basket," TyAnn mentioned.

"What do you mean?" he asked.

"You scored the basket that gave us fifty-one points. They only had fifty for the game. So I figure that your basket was the winning one," TyAnn explained.

Robert didn't quite follow her logic but it didn't matter. They were state champs!

The night at the motel was magical. The boys gathered in Coach's room and stared at the trophy.

"I don't think it will fit in the trophy case, Coach!" Kevin Ambuehl said as he held the trophy.

"We'll have to build a bigger case," Coach Anderson

announced. It was after two in the morning before Robert was able to fall asleep.

In the morning they watched the Lockport team departed for home in their fancy air conditioned Greyhound bus. The Hornets piled into their old school bus for the trip back home. They wouldn't trade places with the Spartans for anything. Fifteen miles outside of town, the highway was lined with cars. Most of the people from town left after the game last night to get back before the team. A few cars had followed them all the way from the Assembly Hall including Mom and Dad. Uncle Charlie and Aunt Mary were riding with them. The boys were all dressed nicely with shirts and ties following Coach's rules. The cheerleaders were allowed to wear their uniforms so TyAnn was wearing hers. She snuck back to sit with Robert, even though Coach usually enforced his rule about the girls staying together at the front of the bus. Coach knew that she was perfectly safe with the boys who were getting louder and louder as they got closer to home—especially the younger kids. The senior group was more subdued. They had worked very hard for four years and were enjoying the moment.

"The younger kids are going to be hard to handle next year," Coach said as he shook his head.

TyAnn found Robert and David sitting together talking about baseball, and who was going to win more games as a pitcher this spring. They had already moved on. TyAnn sat between them and almost on their laps as she listened to them talk about baseball.

"You guys are doofuses," she told them. "You just won the state basketball championship and are talking about baseball already. Can't you take a day or two to enjoy the game?"

Robert looked at David and they grinned mischievously to each other.

TyAnn let out a yell, "Uncle Bill!" as they begin to tickle her.

"Doofuses, huh?" Robert asked. "Is that what we are?"

Uncle Bill turned around, shook his head and muttered, "Kids, God love 'em."

Robert and David stopped teasing TyAnn for a moment. She asked, "Do you think the other team ever caught on to how you guys knew which defense to be in?"

"No, they never had a clue."

On Sunday the town had a parade and at school on Monday they staged a pep rally and canceled the afternoon classes. The recruiters were now after Robert and David even more. They hadn't changed their minds though. They still planned on going to SIU.

Chapter Twenty-Eight

Baseball season started and all of the boys from the basketball team were also on the baseball team, with the exception of Roger Stephens. He had never liked baseball from the time in Little League when he got hit in the side with the ball. After that he was always afraid of getting hit. After he had a growth spurt, he decided that basketball was his game. The guys teased him about not playing baseball, but after they saw him trying to hit the ball during gym class, they were glad he was not on the baseball team. Robert lobbed a few pitches to him, but he didn't come close to hitting the ball.

"You should stick to basketball, Roger. Unless you decide to play on the other team!" Robert teased.

"That's all right with me. I'd rather watch you guys."

Robert and David were the star pitchers. They had a friendly competition between them to see who could strike out the most batters. David led by a slim margin. In early May, the Hornets were playing Patoka City. David was pitching. Dad Benjamin and TyAnn cheered on their team. After the sixth inning, TyAnn mentioned, "Daddy, do you realize that Patoka City doesn't have a hit yet?"

"Are you sure?"

"Yes, I've been keeping track. David walked a guy in the second inning and one in the fifth, but no one has a hit yet."

No one on the bench mentioned that a no-hitter was in progress. It was taboo. In the top of the ninth the Hornets led by five runs. David had still not allowed a hit. He struck out the first batter. The second batter hit a grounder directly at second baseman Rickey Soldner. He fielded the ball cleanly, then as he was about to toss it to Chuck Tomanek at first, he dropped it. The crowd gasped. Rickey picked the ball up. There was still time to throw out the slow runner, but he dropped it again. The runner was safe at first on an error.

"Oh, no. Does that ruin the no-hitter?" TyAnn asked Dad.

"You know better than that. That will be scored an error all the way."

"That's a relief," TyAnn said and then sighed.

On the field Rickey Soldner tossed the ball back to David.

"I'm sorry, David. I just dropped it. I guess I was nervous about the..."

"Don't worry about it. We're still ahead."

David shook off the fielding mistake and struck out the final two batters to complete his no-hitter. The team rushed to him and tackled him to the ground.

"Hey! I don't think we've ever had a no-hitter before," Robert told David.

No one on the team could ever remember being a part of a no-hit game.

"Robert, you're pitching tomorrow against Millstown. Maybe you should throw a no-hitter too," Kevin Ambuehl told him in jest.

"Sure, why not? Maybe I will throw a perfect game just to show I'm a better pitcher than David." Robert knew David was a better pitcher. He forgot all about the joke.

Dad, Mom and TyAnn were in the stands the next afternoon in Millstown.

"Isn't this a beautiful day for a ballgame?" Mom said.

"I heard that Bubby told David he would throw a perfect game today to show who's the best pitcher," TyAnn said.

"That's highly unlikely. Back-to-back no-hitters are extremely rare. I don't think it's ever happened in the majors."

"Well, Bubby can do it."

No one really paid it any attention until the seventh inning. By then the Hornets had a two-run lead thanks to Kevin Ambuehl's two-run homer.

"Daddy, do you know what's..."

"Sssh, baby, you're not supposed to talk about it."

TyAnn smiled at her father, but didn't say anything more. Robert made it through the seventh and eighth innings—still perfect. The Hornets added a run in the top of the ninth to lead by three. Robert took the mound for the bottom of the ninth. His teammates were chattering as usual, but they had not mentioned the perfect game in progress. Robert took his warm-up tosses and settled in to face the lead-off hitter. On the third pitch he hit a screaming line drive. Luckily it was straight at Timmy Crane, the second baseman, who held out his glove and snagged it. It was the hardest hit ball all day for Millstown. Robert struck out the next batter on a called third strike. His thirteenth strikeout of the game. The next batter was Keith Tockstein, the left-handed hitting Millstown first baseman. Robert had struck him out twice already. He took the first pitch for a strike.

"Oh, Daddy, just two more strikes to go. I can't bear to watch." TyAnn closed her eyes and crossed her fingers.

Robert took the sign for the next pitch. He started the wind-up. TyAnn opened her eyes. Tockstein started his swing. The fielders concentrated on the ball. Tockstein made contact. TyAnn heard the sound of the bat hitting the ball. Robert followed the ball as it bounced toward the right side of the diamond.

"Foul ball!" the umpire hollered.

The next two pitches were outside. The count had evened up. Robert took off his cap and wiped his brow. He took the sign from his catcher, Rex Heistand. He started his wind-up. TyAnn kept her eyes open. Dad closed his. Tockstein started the swing. He had been fooled by the off-speed change-up. He made weak contact. The ball blooped in the air between short and third. Kevin Ambuehl had been shaded toward second for the pull hitter. He and Dennis Greenwood, the third baseman, raced for the ball, which was falling faster than a dying quail. Kevin dove and stretched his glove for the ball. The crowd rose to their feet. TyAnn held her breath as she covered her mouth with her hand. Robert turned to look. Tockstein sprinted for first base. The ball kept falling...falling...Kevin stretched an inch more. The ball was almost to the ground. Time stood still for a moment. Then the ball landed. Two inches past the outstretched glove of Kevin. The perfect game disappeared by a matter of inches. Robert shook it off. The next batter hit a lazy fly ball to left on the next pitch. David Tomanek moved three feet to his left and caught it for the last out of the game.

In the car on the way home TyAnn asked, "Are you disappointed, Bubby?"

"Yeah, I suppose I am. I could use the old cliché and say that at least we won the game, but that sounds lame. Just think, a couple inches the other way and Kevin makes the grab. Game over. We win. Perfect game."

"I'm sorry, Bubby."

"I'll get over it," he paused, then laughed. "Wouldn't that have been something though. Back to back no-hitters."

The Hornets had one of their best seasons ever. They only lost two games and those were to much bigger schools. Kevin Ambuehl led the team in batting average and set a school record for the most home runs in a season with ten. Though Robert enjoyed baseball, he realized that basketball was his first love. David had a tougher choice to make. He was as good in baseball as he was in basketball.

Chapter Twenty-Nine

One day as they sat at the dining room table doing homework, TyAnn asked Robert, "Who are you going to ask to the prom?"

"I'm not sure yet," Robert replied. "There aren't many girls to choose from. Most of them already have dates and the ones who don't...Well, let's just say, I won't be asking them."

David had been dating Cathy Terrell, and they planned on going. Chuck and all the rest of the guys from the team had dates already. Robert had always been so involved with sports that he had never had much time for dating. Laurie was his only "girlfriend" so far.

Robert mockingly asked TyAnn, "I suppose you have a date for the prom, huh?"

"As a matter of fact, I do," TyAnn replied smugly.

"Who would be so desperate to ask a freshman to the prom?" Robert wondered out loud.

"I'm not telling," TyAnn said as she escaped to her room.

Robert followed her and closed the door behind him.

"I have ways to make you talk," he threatened.

"Don't you dare. I've got a dress on." TyAnn answered as she scooted back on her bed and wrapped her arms around her knees.

Robert approached her bed slowly pretending to be a diabolical monster about to close in on his prey. TyAnn started laughing and Robert couldn't keep a straight face. He plopped down on the bed beside her as she lay on her back.

"Do you really, really have a date for the prom, or are you just teasing me, Tanny?" he asked quietly.

TyAnn looked at him with hope in her eyes and replied, "I want to go to the prom with you, Bubby. I want you to be my date."

"With me!" Robert exclaimed. "I can't take my little sister to the prom. Everybody will laugh at us, and I'll never be able to live it down."

"Bubby, you are a hero in this town. You could take Charger to the prom, and nobody would say a word," TyAnn said.

"You're too young," Robert replied.

"Are there any rules about how old you have to be to go to the prom?" she asked as she sat up on the bed. "Carolyn Vandermehr went to prom last year when she was only a freshman. I can think of two other freshman girls who are going this year."

"Who?"

"Betty and Sharon Walker are going."

The conversation continued back and forth. Finally, Robert gave in.

"How are you planning on paying for a dress?" Robert asked, hoping she would not have an answer.

"With the money I earned helping Grandma, and the money I got for my birthday, so there."

Robert groaned then said, "All right. If Mom agrees to let you go, I will take you."

She kissed him on the top of his head and dashed into the kitchen to talk to Mom. Robert hid his head in a pillow. "Oh, what have I done? I'll never be able to face my friends again."

"Mom, can I go dancing sometime if Bubby is there to protect and watch after me?" TyAnn asked in a soft voice.

Mom was on the phone and not sure what she had asked, but nodded her head yes. The only words Mom clearly heard were dance, Bubby and protect. TyAnn came running back to her room and told Robert, "Mom said I could go."

"What! Are you kidding me?"

At the supper table that night Mom asked TyAnn, "What were you asking about earlier when I was on the phone with Mrs. Sheffield?"

"Nothing important," TyAnn answered with a guilty look on her face.

Robert stared at her and said, "TyAnn, tell Mom what you were asking about."

TyAnn looked at Mom with her knuckle in her mouth. "I want to go to the prom."

"Tanny, tell Mom the whole story," Robert said as he looked at her sternly.

"Hmmmph!" she exclaimed. "Well, Robert was complaining that he didn't have a date for the prom and knowing how important it is to him since it's his senior year and all, I used my far superior brain and came up with a plan to help him out of his self-imposed predicament by offering to be his date," she rattled off as fast as she could.

Robert looked at her with a blank stare on his face.

"I was only looking out for the best interests of my poor old brother since he is too pathetic to find a date on his own."

"That's very sweet of you," Dad replied.

Mom agreed, "TyAnn, that would be so kind of you to help your brother like that."

Robert shook his head back and forth. "No! This can't be happening. I can't believe you are falling for her story," he told his parents.

Mom asked Robert, "Do you have another date for the prom?"

"Not yet, but I'm working on it," he answered.

TyAnn reminded him, "You said there weren't any girls left worth asking who didn't already have dates. I know for a fact that the only girl left is Priscilla Newcastle, and she is too fat to even dance with."

"TyAnn, that was not a very nice thing to say about someone," Dad scolded.

Robert smirked and Mom even smiled as she thought about Robert trying to dance with Priscilla.

"I'm sorry, but it's true," TyAnn answered with her head down.

Dad asked, "Robert, what do you think about this? Do you even want to go to the prom?"

"I want to go, but I was so busy with basketball and baseball, that I never got around to asking anybody. I guess it's all my fault for waiting so long."

TyAnn looked at her father with hopeful eyes. Dad thought about it for a minute. Dad chuckled softly and announced, "I guess Miss Newcastle wouldn't be very much fun to take to the prom, at that. If you want to let TyAnn go with you, it will be all right with me."

"Oh, thank you, Daddy!" TyAnn shouted as she put her arms around him and gave him a big hug. "I have to call Carolyn and tell her that I have a date to the prom, too."

Robert rolled his eyes and wondered what all his friends were going to think. "I'm going to have to move to Canada and change my name."

Mom helped TyAnn pick out a dress that would be proper and modest enough for a girl of her age. It wasn't easy finding a formal dress to fit her properly, but they found one in a shop in Mount Trenton. TyAnn made Robert practice dancing with her every night the last week before the prom. Robert even complimented her on her dancing ability.

"I AM a cheerleader!" TyAnn reminded him.

The night of the prom arrived and the kids got ready. Robert looked so handsome in his tux, and TyAnn looked very pretty in her new dress. She didn't have her hair in a ponytail like she normally did. Robert even had a corsage for TyAnn to wear.

"Do I have to pin it on her?" Robert complained.

"I will take care of that for you," Mom answered as she helped him out of a sticky situation. Mom took pictures of them.

Dad asked in a stern voice, "Young man, what time do you plan on having my daughter back tonight?"

"Oh, Daddy!" TyAnn said and then giggled.

Dad laughed as Robert and TyAnn headed out the door. Mom hollered at them, "Have fun!"

Robert didn't know what to expect when they got there. He had not told anyone about taking TyAnn, except for David. They walked to the gym and TyAnn held onto Robert's arm as they entered. David and Cathy had arrived ten minutes earlier, and they came over to greet Robert and TyAnn. They mingled with the other kids and nobody teased Robert about his "date." When the dancing started, Robert hesitated at first to dance with her.

"Come on, Bubby," she whispered. "I want to dance with you."

After seeing TyAnn dance, David and some of the other basketball players asked her to dance, as well. Even Roger Stephens danced with her. It was comical to Robert to watch Roger, at six-seven, dance with his little sister. At ten o'clock the band took a break. When they came back on stage, the new king and queen were crowned. No one seemed to be surprised when Kevin Ambuehl and Laurie Roland took their places for the photographer. Even though the prom lasted much longer, by midnight TyAnn was ready to go home. Robert told his friends good night and he and TyAnn headed home.

Mom and Dad were waiting up to ask about their night.

TyAnn told them in a dreamy voice, "It was perfect. I danced with so many different boys, but no one could dance like Bubby."

She headed to her room to get ready for bed. Robert sat with Mom and Dad for awhile.

Mom asked, "Did your friends tease you about your date?"

Robert shook his head and replied, "Nobody even seemed to pay any attention to me being there with TyAnn. She danced with some of the other guys, and sometimes the girls would dance together. I think we both had a good time."

He went to his room to get ready for bed and found TyAnn, already in her pajamas, waiting to talk to him. He took off his jacket, tie and shoes and sat on the side of the bed. "My feet are killing me. I'm glad I don't have to wear those shoes all the time. My back hurts, too."

"Do you need a back massage, old man?" TyAnn teased. She rubbed his back and shoulders. "Thank you for taking me tonight. I had so much fun and felt so grown up."

"You're welcome, Tanny. I hate to admit it, but I'm glad I took you because I had fun, too. If I had been with any of those other girls, I would had been uncomfortable knowing I was there with them, but that I didn't really like them as a girlfriend or anything."

"Are you sad you didn't get to kiss a girl good night."

"No, not really because girls are...icky!" Robert said as he turned to tickle her.

She laughed and giggled as Robert tormented her. Dad hollered at them, "Knock it off in there. Mom and I are going to bed."

TyAnn ran out to give Mom a hug and get a good night kiss from Dad.

"Good night, baby," Mom said.

After Robert came back to his room from the bathroom, TyAnn was waiting on his bed for him with Charger.

"I'm not tired anymore," she said. She was quiet for a moment, then asked, "What am I going to do next year when you are gone?"

The only time they had spent more than a couple nights apart in their whole lives was when she was in the hospital. They spent an hour quietly talking to each other until she fell asleep.

"Well, Charger, I guess it will be up to you to take care of her next year."

Charger wagged her tail as Robert carried TyAnn to her room.

Chapter Thirty

During the summer after TyAnn had reached her fourth birthday, she had asked Mom, "Can I get a puppy to play with?"

"Why do you want a puppy?" Mom asked.

"I want to have somebody to play with while Bubby is at school."

Mom and Dad discussed the matter and decided to find a puppy for the family. They knew of a local farmer who had a new litter of Labrador retrievers. Mom and Dad took TyAnn and Robert out to see the puppies one Saturday morning. TyAnn was on her knees as she looked at the six puppies, who played in their pen, and wanted to take all of them home.

"Can we keep all the puppies?"

"We can only have one puppy," Dad said.

She couldn't make up her mind. Dad thought the largest puppy, a yellow lab, would be a good choice to maybe train as a hunting dog for he and his brother. The farmer let the puppies out of their pen and immediately the smallest one scampered over to TyAnn, knocked her down and began licking her face.

The farmer laughed as he told Dad, "Did you see the way that little runt charged at her!"

TyAnn had made her choice, or did the puppy choose TyAnn? Either way, the decision was made.

"What do you want to name your puppy?" Dad asked.

"Charger!" she replied immediately, "because of what the farmer said."

And so Charger came to live with them in town.

Charger learned how to fetch a ball and followed TyAnn everywhere. Charger even learned how to find "Doll Kitty" and bring her to TyAnn. When Robert walked to school in the morning, TyAnn and Charger were allowed to walk along to the last block before the "busy" street where the school was located. TyAnn and Charger were not allowed to cross that street. Although the school was only a block and a half from home, to TyAnn it seemed a long way away. Charger developed a life-long habit of walking the kids to school. Charger also seemed to be able to tell time because she knew just when Robert was supposed to be coming home and waited for him on the corner. Charger loved to visit the farm with the family. Charger would take off and run through the woods and loved to swim in the pond. One day while going fishing with Robert and Dad, TyAnn dropped her Doll Kitty on the way to the pond. She didn't realize it until it was time to head back.

"Where is Doll Kitty? I can't find Doll Kitty!" TyAnn started to cry.

"Are you sure you had her with you?" Robert asked.

Dad knew TyAnn always had Doll Kitty with her. Charger came over to see why TyAnn was crying.

"Charger, go find Doll Kitty!" Robert said. Charger wagged her tail as Robert repeated the command, "Go find Doll Kitty."

Charger took off running toward the the barnyard. Charger circled around out of sight for a moment and soon reappeared with Doll Kitty held gently in her mouth. TyAnn saw her precious doll, hugged Charger and held her tight.

Charger became an important part of the family and was even allowed to sleep in the house. Charger slept on the floor in the kid's room. Robert and TyAnn learned how to be responsible for feeding her and making sure Charger had enough water. They even got up to let Charger outside in the morning. Charger became a good watch dog and was very protective of TyAnn and Robert, but especially TyAnn. When Robert tickled TyAnn, Charger came over to make sure she was all right. Charger was very gentle with the kids and TyAnn often fell asleep with her head on Charger, using her as a pillow. When TyAnn was in kindergarten, Charger made an extra trip to the corner. TyAnn skipped home with Charger after school, and they played outside all afternoon.

One day a stranger meandered into the back yard. TyAnn didn't notice him and Mom was busy inside doing the dishes. The man started talking to TyAnn after coming within a few yards of her. Charger started growling and sat in front of TyAnn. When the man took another step toward TyAnn, Charger began to bark loudly. She stood up and moved toward the man. Mom heard the barking and walked to the back door. She saw the man and opened the door. The stranger turned and walked away. Mom called the local police officer, and told him about the man in the back yard. As it turned out, the man was a friend of Dad's from the insurance company he worked for in the summer. The man came back to the house later after Dad was home from school. His name was Fred McDowell, and Dad introduced him to everyone, including Charger. Charger was still wary of him and kept herself between Mr. McDowell and TyAnn.

Over the years Charger became a familiar sight around town as she accompanied the kids everywhere. Charger went to baseball games and fetched foul balls that got lost in the weeds. TyAnn thought that Charger even barked at the umpire if he made a "bad call" against the home team. During one game Charger barked several times at close calls and the umpire, Kevin Ambuehl's father, LaVerne, came over to talk to Charger.

"Charger, I will throw you out of the game if you don't stop arguing with my calls."

TyAnn grinned as she told Mr. Ambuehl, "If you throw Charger out, you will have to throw me out, too."

"Honey, I won't throw you out. I was just teasing Charger," Mr. Ambuehl said as he smiled and patted Charger on the head.

When the game ended on a questionable called third strike against the home team, TyAnn looked at Charger. Charger put her paw over her eyes and sat quietly.

Chapter Thirty-One

Senior trips had been a tradition at the school for many years, and this year's graduating class had worked hard raising money for this year's adventure. They had held fundraisers all throughout their years in high school toward this week. One of the best money makers was a car wash held early in September of Robert's senior year. The weather cooperated and the kids had a beautiful Saturday for the car wash. All the kids dressed casually in shorts and t-shirts. TyAnn helped Robert and a dozen other seniors as they washed cars all morning and into the afternoon.

"I'm starving," Robert told TyAnn.

"Daddy, can I run home to get the cooler?"

Mr. Benjamin, the faculty sponsor for the senior class, had been supervising the car wash. "Yeah, go ahead and take Robert to help you."

"I don't need his help. I will use the wagon to carry the cooler." She hurried home and bolted into the house. "Mom, are the sandwiches ready?" she asked still out of breath.

"Everything is ready to go, and the cooler is all packed," Mom answered.

Mom helped TyAnn load the old red Radio Flyer Wagon, and TyAnn and Charger headed back to the school. There were sandwiches, pop and even some homemade cookies for all the kids working in the hot sun. Everyone took a break, as there were no customers at the time. After eating, several more customers appeared and the kids were busy again. Finally, things slowed down and the car wash appeared to be finished. It seemed as if everyone in Kinmundy Junction, who had a car, had been there today. Even Mr. Bilek brought his thirty-year-old pick-up truck to town to be washed. Most of the kids left to go home and only Robert, David and TyAnn were left to help Dad with the final car —their own. TyAnn was manning the water hose watching Charger when Robert came around the corner of the car. She wasn't looking and accidentally got him "slightly" wet.

"Oh, Bubby, I'm sorry. I didn't mean it," TyAnn said.

"That's what you said the last time!" Robert looked at her with a devilish grin on his face.

This wasn't the first time today TyAnn had "accidentally"

gotten him wet.

"Daddy!" she screamed as Robert and David caught her before she could get away.

Dad had seen everything and smiled. He was inclined to let the kids enjoy some fun and told TyAnn, "You started the spraying and now you have to pay for it."

Robert and David each had a hose in their hands now and she was trapped. She ran around the car and Robert let her have it full blast. She was soaked and scrambled around the other direction to run into David, and he sprayed her also. Dad wondered why TyAnn kept running around the car and not away from the boys. She was having too much fun, and the cold water felt so good on the hot sunny day. She stopped running and laid on her back on the hood of the car. Robert came over with his hose.

"I give up. I surrender," she said as she tried to catch her breath. Robert set the hose to mist and sprayed her one final time.

The senior trip that year was to Daytona Beach, Florida. As part of his duties as the senior class sponsor, Dad accompanied the class on the trip. Mom and TyAnn were planning to stay home, but at the last minute, space on the bus opened up, and they were able to go along. The first stop was an overnight stay in Macon, Georgia. Early in the afternoon of the second day, the bus pulled in to the motel in St. Augustine, Florida. They spent some time visiting the "Old Fort" and the "Fountain of Youth."

The next day the bus made it to Daytona Beach, where they would spend the rest of the week. For most of the kids it was their first time in Florida. In fact many of them had never been any farther away from home than St. Louis or Chicago. The bus took them to the Daytona Speedway, and they got to take a couple of laps around the famous racetrack. Some of the kids took a ride in a glass-bottomed boat and saw many different species of fish beneath them. Robert threatened to throw TyAnn overboard, but Dad made him behave. TyAnn made fun of Robert and he warned her, "Just wait 'til later, little sister. Dad can't be watching you all the time. He has to keep an eye on the other kids, too."

"I'm not afraid of you!" TyAnn said as she hid behind David.

Most of the rest of the time in Daytona Beach, the kids were free to explore the beaches and shops along the street where the hotel was located. TyAnn was safe at night in her room with Mom and Dad, but during the day she was fair game for Robert and David.

David and his girlfriend, Cathy, hung out with Robert and TyAnn on the beach almost all the time. Chuck and his girlfriend, Teresa Garrett, spent a lot of time with them, also. Robert let TyAnn bury him in sand, and they had fun like when they were very young. They went swimming in the ocean, and Robert teased her and threw her around in the water.

After dinner one night back at the hotel, Robert, TyAnn, David and Cathy were sitting by the pool in their shorts and t-shirts.

"I wish we didn't have to leave tomorrow," TyAnn said.

"We could just leave you here," Robert teased her.

"You would miss me too much. Who would you have to tease if I wasn't there?" TyAnn replied.

David and Cathy sat and listened to them bickering and teasing each other. They were used to their antics. David leaned over to kiss Cathy while TyAnn was watching.

"I'm telling," TyAnn threatened David.

David told her, "Go ahead, we are allowed to kiss each other. WE are not a child like YOU," David teased her.

"I'm not a child!" TyAnn retorted.

"Yes you are," Robert replied as he laughed at her. "You're still wet behind the ears."

"Am not, I'm more mature than you were when you were my age. What do you mean 'wet behind the ears,' anyway? What kind of old-fashioned doofus answer is that. I'm not wet anywhere."

TyAnn told them with feigned fierceness and a little trepidation in her voice. With a mischievous gleam in his eye Robert told her, "You'll be wet soon enough, and not just behind your ears, either."

Robert and David looked at each other knowing what each other was thinking. They stood up.

She looked at them and meekly begged them, "Oh, no, don't you dare. You better not. I'll tell Mom."

But it was of no use. Robert grabbed her and put her over his shoulder. She continued to plead and tried to bargain with Robert.

"I'll do your chores for a week. I'll clean your room. I'll do anything."

David followed along. Cathy grabbed a towel and smiled. Robert and David grabbed her ankles and her hands and swung her back and forth.

"On the count of three," Robert told David.

"One...Two...Three!"

TyAnn screamed as she went flying high in the air, and out into the pool. She made a huge splash, for an under-ninety-pound girl, and swam over to the side of the pool. Robert grinned as he held out his hand to help her get out.

"Thanks, Bubby," TyAnn said as she reached for his hand.

She placed her feet on the pool wall, grabbed his hand and pulled with all her might. Robert lost his balance and toppled into the pool.

"Now who's wet behind the ears?" TyAnn mockingly told him as she climbed out. Robert climbed out of the pool with a grin on his face and TyAnn noticed.

"Bubby, I'm already soaked. I can get any wetter," She shouted as Robert held her around her waist as he carried her close to the pool again.

Robert threatened to toss her in again, but he didn't. He sat on the edge of the pool with her. "Tanny, you're still my best friend," he said quietly as they sat next to each other.

The next day the bus began the long trip back to Kinmundy Junction, and the final few days of school.

Chapter Thirty-Two

After graduation, Robert and David were busy working on the farm with Grandpa. Grandpa Tomanek, now eighty-six years old, had gotten to the point that he needed help to maintain the farm. For the Fourth of July the whole family gathered at the farm for a cookout. Everyone was there: Mom and Dad with Robert and TyAnn; Uncle Charlie, Aunt Mary and their sons Steve, Mark and David; Aunt Marie and Coach Anderson, Uncle Bill, were there. They had no kids of their own but loved to spoil all their nieces and nephews. The older siblings were there also. Uncle August, who everyone called Gus, and Aunt Viola with their two kids, Dwayne and Ed. Dwayne's wife Donna and newborn son, Isaac, were there, too. Uncle Frank and Aunt Barbara were there with Chuck and Barbara's kids from her first marriage, Tom, Jimmy and Andy Wilson. Grandma wanted to get a picture of her and Grandpa and all the kids. Dad agreed to take the picture. Grandma and Grandpa sat in chairs with all their kids standing behind them. The kids lined up according to their age. Gus was on the left since he was the oldest. Marie was next, followed by Charlie. Frank stood next to Grandpa and Emma next to him, the youngest of the kids. Dad took two pictures just to be sure, then the whole family got together for a picture. Mr. Polanka agreed to take the picture for them. The whole family stood close to the front porch of the old farm house. It became a very cherished picture for the family, and in later years copies were made for all the family members. It was the last picture ever taken with everybody all together.

Three weeks later, Uncle Charlie found Grandpa in his workshop, sitting on the cold hard floor. Adolphus Tomanek's heart had finally given out after working so hard for so many years. The wake and funeral were held in town at the Linville-Bailey Funeral Home. TyAnn spent most of the time sitting next to Grandma.

Grandma held onto TyAnn's hand as she reminisced. "I remember when your mom and dad brought you home from the hospital. You had curly brown hair and looked so much like your mother. Your parents stopped at the farmhouse on your way home. I got to hold you while you were sleeping. Grandpa was thrilled to have a granddaughter. He held you in his arms and stared at you." Grandma paused for a moment and wiped away some tears. "You woke up and looked at him. He claims you smiled at him, but I know you couldn't really see him. He kissed your forehead and made funny noises at you. He never did that with any of the other grandchildren."

After the funeral service, a small caravan of cars, and one very old pick-up truck, made their way out of town. They crossed the river, and drove slowly past the farm. They continued west past the old Williams' homestead and down the hill into Bilek's Bottoms. TyAnn remembered when several years ago, the entire area had been under water. The procession turned and headed south on Bilek Road, then east on Hicks Road. Martin Cemetery was situated on top of the hill at the end of the road. It had been started in the 1850s and was named for one of the founders of Almaville, John Martin.

After the graveside ceremony, Robert and TyAnn strolled around the old cemetery.

TyAnn spotted an old headstone. "Look, Bubby, this one is from 1853. You can barely make out the date."

Robert followed as she sauntered through the oldest section of the small cemetery. TyAnn found one gravesite where a couple of weeds had sprouted. She knelt down to pull them and noticed the name on the marker.

"Look, Bubby, this one says Josef Polanka. I remember that name, but this one died in 1940."

"You are thinking about his son, most likely. His name is Joe. He is the guy who took the picture of the family on the Fourth."

"I wondered who that was."

"Mom told me once that he and Grandpa were cousins. Joe and Linnie, that's his wife, live in that house across the road and down a little ways from Uncle Charlie."

"I remember going over there once when I was a little girl."

"You're still a little girl, Tanny," Robert teased.

"Am not! I'm fifteen now."

"You still act like you're ten."

"If I wasn't so mature and wearing a dress, I would chase you back to the car."

They sauntered back and rejoined the rest of the family.

David asked, "Where did you guys go? Grandma was looking for you, Ty."

"We were looking at some of the headstones. I'll go see what Grandma wants." TyAnn walked over to Grandma's side and put her arm through hers. "I'm back, Grandma. Bubby and I were looking at some of the other graves. Do you need anything?"

"No, I'm all right. I didn't know where you were."

"I'll stay with you now, Grandma."

The family made their way back into Kinmundy Junction. The Methodist church had a meal for the family. When that was finished Mom and Dad were going to take Grandma back to the farm.

"Would it be all right if I spend a couple weeks with Grandma?" TyAnn asked.

Mom answered, "That would be very thoughtful of you, sweetie. Are you sure you want to?"

"Yes, and I promise I won't cause her any extra work." TyAnn packed a suitcase and stayed with Grandma for the next two weeks.

Chapter Thirty-Three

The rest of the summer of '65 flew by and Robert and David were soon ready to head to Southern Illinois University. Robert loaded up the car for the trip. Mom and Dad were sad to see him leave but realized Robert was growing up. Uncle Charlie, Aunt Mary and David met them in their car, and they traveled to Carbondale together. On the way, Robert sat in the backseat with TyAnn, who for some reason was being very quiet on the trip. Not her normal chatterbox at all.

"Are you okay, Tanny? You seem awful quiet for some reason."

"I'm fine. I was just thinking about something."

Robert knew something was bothering her, but she wouldn't tell him what. He didn't think it was about his leaving for college because she had been teasing him all summer about using his bedroom as a guest room for her girlfriends. As they got closer to Carbondale, TyAnn reached over and held Robert's hand. She had promised herself that she would not cry. Over and over she told herself, "I will not cry, I will not cry."

When they reached the campus, it was a madhouse. Hundreds of new freshman rushed about everywhere. Robert and David were sharing a room in the freshman dorm Foster Hall. They managed to find their room and unloaded the cars. Everybody wanted to grab some dinner before heading home. They found a restaurant nearby called the Saluki Diner.

"What's a Saluki?" TyAnn asked.

Robert explained patiently, "A Saluki was a Royal Egyptian dog, and is one of the oldest breeds of dogs."

TyAnn looked at him, as if he had two heads, as Robert rattled on about what he had learned about Salukis.

"What on earth does that had to do with SIU?" TyAnn asked after Robert finished.

Dad explained to her that southern Illinois was sometimes called Little Egypt. Dad said, "The teams were called the Maroons when I went to school here."

"Why can't they have a normal name like Hornets or something?" TyAnn wondered aloud.

The seven of them finished dinner, and soon the parents

121

needed to head home.

"I will not cry, I will not cry," TyAnn whispered under her breath.

David said goodbye to his parents and headed up to the room. Mom and Dad Benjamin said goodbye and Mom hugged Robert.

"Remember how I told you to separate your clothes when you do laundry and try to get enough sleep."

"I will, Mom."

Dad shook his hand, then gave Robert a hug, also. "Call if you need anything, son."

"I will. David and I will do okay. We kinda know our way around the campus already."

Robert looked at TyAnn. She held her arms up in the air and Robert picked her up off the ground and held her tight. Her tears started flowing immediately.

"Oh, Bubby, I tried not to cry," TyAnn whispered.

"It's okay, Tanny," Robert said softly as his eyes got misty. "I will miss you. You can come to a football game and we will see each other soon."

Robert put her down and went inside. TyAnn sat quietly in the backseat on the way home. Mom knew it would probably be harder for her to adjust to Robert being away than it would be for him. Robert and David adjusted to campus life and soon settled into a routine. Robert knew he wanted to become a coach, but David hadn't made up his mind whether to become a doctor or a teacher.

A month later Robert and David caught the train and came home for a visit. The train made a special stop in Kinmundy Junction to drop them off. They arrived early Friday afternoon while everyone was still at school. Mom and Dad knew they were coming, but Robert wanted to surprise TyAnn. Robert and David walked the couple blocks from the station to the house.

"It feels good to be back home. I don't mind admitting that I kinda miss the place. Carbondale seems so big compared to here," Robert said.

"Just think how I must feel," David joked. "I grew up in the country. At least you live in town."

Robert noticed that the old mulberry tree was not nearly as big as he remembered as a kid. He looked to his left and chuckled as he remembered the old black tarpaper shack that used to scare TyAnn. It had been gone for several years now. Robert had time to run David out to the farm before anyone got home from school. When they arrived, Uncle Charlie was out in the field working, but Aunt Mary was home. She had made a German chocolate cake for David and offered Robert a piece.

"I just finished frosting it. Would you like a piece."

"Thanks, Aunt Mary. I don't mind if I have a slice."

"You can take some home, if you like."

"Sure, if David and Uncle Charlie don't mind."

"There will be plenty left for them."

TyAnn was busy after school with a FHA, Future Housewives of America, meeting. Robert got back from Uncle Charlie's farm and waited in his room with Charger for TyAnn to get home. TyAnn wondered why Charger didn't meet her as she started walking home. Charger usually knew to wait for her. She hurried home, entered through the back door and hollered, "Mom, I'm home! Charger, where are you?"

TyAnn heard Charger barking in Robert's room and stepped into the room looking for her. She saw Charger standing on the bed wagging her tail furiously.

"Why didn't you meet me at the corner?" TyAnn asked Charger as Robert snuck up behind her. He grabbed her around her waist and lifted her high in the air.

"Bubby!" she screamed.

Robert set her down, and she turned to face him. "When did you get home? How long can you stay? How is school?"

TyAnn asked a thousand other questions, all as fast as she could talk. She jumped on the bed with Charger, and Robert sat on the edge and told her all about school.

Mom called, "Supper is ready. Come and get it."

At the table TyAnn had so many questions about school, that it took Robert twice as long as normal to eat his supper.

"TyAnn, why don't you let your brother eat, then you two can talk all you want about school."

"Okay, I just wanted to hear everything about college life. Do you have a girlfriend yet?"

123

Robert poked her in the ribs. "No, I've been too busy to worry about a girlfriend."

"Please tell me you have at least noticed there are girls on campus. I will worry about you otherwise."

"I have noticed there are girls, and some of them are really cute. They are also much more mature than you."

"I would hope so, doofus. I'm only fifteen, you know."

"I seem to remember you telling me how mature you were because you were fifteen. Now you're trying to tell me the opposite. Which is it?"

"I am not getting into a discussion with you about my maturity. So there!" She made a face at him and stuck out her tongue.

Dad laughed and said, "Now this is how I remember supper being. It's been much to quiet around here lately."

Robert and TyAnn finished eating, and she followed him into his room. She plopped on his bed while he unpacked his small suitcase.

"How is the food? Do they have anything good at the cafeteria?"

"It's not like Mom's or Grandma's cooking, but it's all right. David and I aren't starving yet."

TyAnn stayed in Robert's room until midnight when he chased her out so he could go to bed.

"I'll see you in the morning, TyAnn. I'm going to sleep now. We can do something together tomorrow if you want."

"Can we go into Millstown. I think they are playing football tomorrow against... I forget who they're playing, but could we go?"

"Sure, if you want. Now go to bed!"

"Night, Bubby. I'm glad you're home."

Chapter Thirty-Four

Saturday morning TyAnn woke up early and peeked in Robert's room. "I think he's still asleep, Charger. He probably doesn't get enough sleep at school. We should let him sleep. Let's eat breakfast."

TyAnn and Charger headed to the kitchen. Robert was listening to TyAnn, but he was really tired and appreciated her concern over his lack of sleep. He slept for two more hours, then got up.

"'Bout time you got up, sleepyhead. The day's half gone!"

"It's only 9:30, Tanny. What are you eating?"

"Yogurt! Want some?"

"No, thanks! When did you start eating yogurt?" Robert asked.

"Since I had some at Carolyn's house. It's good for you."

Robert took a bite and made a face. TyAnn giggled at him.

"What are we going to do today, Bubby?"

"Do you still want to see the football game?"

"Sure, if you don't mind. Maybe David and Cathy will go with us. I'll call him and see."

TyAnn called and talked to Aunt Mary.

"He went over to her house, TyAnn. You could call over there, and ask them what they were planning to do today."

"Okay, thanks. Oh, the cake was delicious. Robert didn't eat it all, so I had a piece. Thanks, Aunt Mary."

"You're welcome, sweetheart."

TyAnn called and finally got to talk to David. "Do you guys want to go with me and Robert to watch the game in Millstown?"

"That sounds like fun. We were trying to decide what to do. How about I pick you guys up around noon, and we can grab a bite to eat, then catch the game."

"Sounds like a plan. We'll be ready."

David and Cathy stopped over a few minutes after noon. Robert and TyAnn were ready and waiting.

"Hi, Cathy! How have you been?"

"Good, how is school this year, Ty?"

"All right, but kinda boring so far."

"Well, college is kinda boring too if you have to live at home and commute to Kaskaskia, like I do."

They piled in the car and headed out. They stopped at the Wildcat Cafe to grab a quick lunch before heading over to the football field. The first game was starting the third quarter. They watched the end of that game, then watched the varsity play.

"It's too bad we don't have a football team," TyAnn told Robert.

"You would make a good quarterback, Tanny!"

"Oh, yeah, right! Can you see me in the huddle with a bunch of huge guys around me?"

"Where would you get a bunch of huge guys in town?"

"I guess that's why we don't have a football team. Forget I ever said anything."

They watched the rest of the game, then decided to stop and see Grandma.

Grandma was out in the yard when they pulled up in front.

"Hi, Grandma!" TyAnn yelled as she got out of the car.

Grandma saw TyAnn, Robert and David and smiled. She recognized Cathy Terrell as being David's girlfriend, but couldn't remember her name. "I am glad to see you boys. Will you do something for me?"

"Of course, Grandma. What do you need us to do?" Robert asked.

"I can't get the gate by the machine shed closed all the way. Will you take a look at it for me."

The guys took a look at the gate and discovered a couple loose bolts. In no time the gate was repaired. Robert realized that Grandma needed helped with the farm since Grandpa was gone now. He asked Grandma, "Is there anything else you need done?"

"You boys don't need to do anything," Grandma said.

"We don't mind, Grandma. Just tell us what you need done. We really don't mind."

Grandma mentioned a few more things and the kids got to work. Even Cathy pitched in to help and soon they had completed everything.

"Thank you for taking care of that for me. Now you relax, and I'll make some supper for us."

TyAnn helped Grandma make supper, and they all sat

down in the kitchen and ate. Grandma sat quietly, and listened to the kids as they talked and teased each other. After the kitchen was cleaned, the kids were ready to head home.

"Thanks for supper, Grandma," TyAnn said.

"You're welcome. Thank you for all the work you did."

Everyone hugged Grandma, even Cathy, and they left.

"Do you think Grandma gets lonely now that Grandpa is gone?" Robert asked.

"I'm sure she does at times," David answered. "But her kids stop by as much as they can."

David dropped Robert and TyAnn off, then took Cathy home.

Robert mentioned to Dad what they did at the farm. "We had to pry the information out of Grandma to know what needed to be fixed."

"I guess we will have to pay closer attention to the farm now. Grandma never asks us to do anything. I think we will have to inspect the farm and take care of repairs as we see them."

Sunday afternoon Robert caught the train back to school. TyAnn walked with him up the hill to the station.

"Do you want to come to a football game next Saturday, Tanny?"

"Sure!" TyAnn answered as her eyes lit up. "I've never seen a college football game, except maybe on TV."

They talked about the game while Robert waited for the train. Uncle Charlie dropped David off at the station.

He saw TyAnn, "Hello, little lady. How are you today?"

"I'm fine, Uncle Charlie. How are you feeling today, and how is Aunt Mary?"

"We are both doing well. Say hi to your mom and dad for me. I've got to get back to the farm."

TyAnn sat with Robert and David on a bench outside the station as they waited for the train to arrive.

"How have classes been?"

"Classes? Shoot! I knew there was something I forgot to do," Robert suddenly remembered.

"What did you forget?" TyAnn asked.

"I forgot to go to my classes. I suppose I should start doing

127

that."

TyAnn shook her head. "Don't bother now, doofus."

TyAnn heard the train coming. It came to a gradual stop and Robert and David grabbed their bags and got ready to board.

"Don't forget about the football game on Saturday, Tanny. I'll talk to you during the week. See ya later."

TyAnn waited until Robert and David were on the train, and she saw them sit down. The train took off and she waved goodbye. She waited until the train was out of sight, then walked home.

Chapter Thirty-Five

Robert called on Wednesday and talked to TyAnn about the weekend.

"Will you be all right riding the train by yourself?" Robert asked, knowing it would get a reaction from her.

"I'm not a baby anymore. I'm fifteen. In another year I will be able to drive to Carbondale if I want. Not that I would want to see you."

On Friday afternoon TyAnn caught the train, and Robert met her at the station in Carbondale. He had arranged for her to stay with cousin Dwayne and his family, who lived on a farm only ten miles away. Dwayne met Robert and TyAnn for supper, then took TyAnn home with him. TyAnn got to hold baby Isaac again. She even changed a diaper. Saturday morning Dwayne brought her to campus, and she met up with Robert and David.

"Can I see your room?" TyAnn asked Robert.

"Girls aren't allowed in the building," Robert said with a wink at David. "You can see it on Family Day with Mom and Dad."

"Show me where your classes are then."

Robert took her on a tour of campus, and she was in awe of all the many buildings and the students.

"I'm going to go to school here when I graduate," TyAnn announced to Robert proudly. She sat with Robert and David at the football game and cheered loudly for the Salukis. Unfortunately they lost the game to Eastern Illinois, but she didn't mind too much since Robert and David weren't on the team. TyAnn spent another night with Dwayne and he brought her back to town on Sunday morning. She had lunch with Robert and David, then caught the train for home.

Mom, Dad and TyAnn returned to campus later for Family Day. Uncle Charlie and Aunt Mary rode down to Carbondale with them. This time TyAnn got to see Robert and David's dorm room.

"Which bed is yours, Bubby? Oh nevermind, it must be this one. I can tell because you have never been able to make your bed very neatly," TyAnn teased.

"Aren't you so funny!?"

"Have you gone to any classes this week?" she asked.

"I went to one class in the math building, but it was the wrong one. Maybe someday I will learn where my classes are."

TyAnn looked at David and shook her head. "He is hopeless. Have you met any cute girls yet?"

"Hundreds of them! There are so many good looking girls here," Robert answered.

"Did you ask anyone out for a date yet? You are old enough to date now, you know."

"Thank you for your permission. Now I feel so much better."

David laughed and said, "He likes this girl in his Algebra class, but he is too shy to talk to her."

"Bubby, why don't you talk to her. You don't need to be shy. Is she cute? What's her name?" TyAnn asked.

"I don't know her name. There are too many kids in class to learn everyone's name."

"You don't need to learn everyone's name, just one certain girl. Just go up to her and ask her her name. You do know how to talk, right?"

They ate dinner in the cafeteria. After dinner, TyAnn stayed with Robert and David in their room.

Mom and Dad took Charlie and Mary on a walk around the campus. Dad remarked to Mom, "There are a few new buildings, but I remember most of the older ones."

"I lived in that dorm for two years," Mom said.

"That used to be the math building." Dad pointed out one of the older buildings.

"The new student center is nice."

Both Mom and Dad attended college here. They pointed out all the buildings they remembered to Charlie and Mary. They finished their tour of the campus and returned to the dorm.

"We should get over to the motel. Are you ready, TyAnn?"

They had reserved two rooms at the Saluki Inn.

"Can I stay here with Robert and David? I won't have any fun at the motel."

"Of course not! That would not be proper for a young lady," Mom admonished her.

"Oh, Mom," TyAnn said slowly.

"I'll see you in the morning, Ty. We aren't allowed to have girls spend the night, even though you are my sister."

"See you guys later," TyAnn told them as she left their room.

They had breakfast together, then the parents needed to get back home. Mom and Dad talked to Robert for a few minutes, then he walked over to TyAnn.

"Thanks for letting me see your room."

"You can see it anytime you come to visit, Ty. I was teasing you the last time you were here."

"I know you were. I'm not that dumb!"

Chapter Thirty-Six

At the beginning of her sophomore year, TyAnn had somehow managed to squeeze more hours into her busy day. She seemed even more active in school activities than last year. Besides being a cheerleader and involved with her after-school activities, the school paper and the yearbook, she was involved with both school plays. She thought about someday making a career on the stage in some capacity.

One afternoon in early November TyAnn stepped out of her Geometry class and found Brent Gentry waiting for her by her locker.

"Hi, Brent, what's up?"

"Uh, I was kinda wondering if you were... uh... do you... well... do you have a date for homecoming already?" He finally managed to blurt out.

"No, I don't. I guess I never really thought about it. Why?" She knew he wanted to ask her to go with him, but she enjoyed prolonging his discomfort.

"I was wondering if you would go with me?"

"You mean like on a real date?" She could barely keep a straight face as he blushed. She could see beads of sweat popping out on his forehead.

"Well, yeah, I guess it would be like a real date. You don't have to kiss me or nothing. I swear I wouldn't try to kiss you."

"Hmmmm, I suppose I could. No, wait. That's the night of the... No, that's the following week." She was enjoying seeing Brent squirm. "Okay, I'll go to homecoming with you." She accepted his offer partly because she thought he was about to pass out.

When Robert learned about her homecoming date, he teased her, "Are you sure he wants to go with you? Maybe he meant to ask one of the Walker sisters, but got the wrong number."

"Very funny! He didn't ask over the phone. He asked me in person. I feel kinda bad now because I sorta strung him along. I finally agreed because he was sweating so much I thought he was about to have a stroke. Are you coming to homecoming?"

"David and I are both coming. We want to see you and

Brent dancing together."

"He is probably a klutz with three left feet."

By the time Robert got home from Carbondale, Brent had already picked TyAnn up. Robert changed clothes and hurried down to the gym. The varsity game had just started when he found a seat. TyAnn saw him and rushed over to talk even though the cheerleaders were supposed to be doing a routine.

"It's about time you got here. I was starting to believe you weren't coming."

"Now, would I miss seeing my little sister on the night of her first date," he teased.

"You better be nice to me."

"I seem to remember a young girl teasing me about my first date." Robert smiled because he was about to get his revenge.

"I have to go. I'll talk to you after the game. I have to run home."

"Why?"

"Because I'm not going to the dance in my cheerleader uniform, doofus."

After the game, which the Hornets won by fifteen points over LaGrove, Robert had a chance to talk with his teammates from the previous year. Chuck Tomanek was attending Eastern Illinois. Kevin Ambuehl had decided on McKendree College. Roger Stephens chose Kaskaskia Junior College where he could play basketball. The rest of the guys from the team were still in high school, including Brent Gentry. Robert saw him after he had showered and changed.

"Hi, Brent, good game."

"Thanks, Robert. We aren't as good as you guys were last year. Last year might be the highlight of my life. I'll never forget the state tournament as long as I live." Brent looked around trying to locate someone.

"TyAnn hustled home to change. She should be back in a few minutes."

"Thanks," Brent answered nervously. "I hope you don't mind that I asked TyAnn to the dance."

"Not at all. I hope you guys have fun." Robert noticed that beads of sweat were already appearing on Brent's forehead.

TyAnn made it back a few minutes later. She saw Robert talking to David and Chuck and strolled over. "Have you seen Brent around?"

"I saw him standing by the stage a couple minutes ago," David replied.

"I better go find him. He's supposed to be my date. I'll talk to you guys later."

An hour later Robert saw TyAnn sitting alone on the first row of bleachers. "Would you like to dance, Tanny?"

"Yes, Brent is a terrible dancer. I think my feet are both bruised from him stepping on me so many times."

TyAnn and Robert danced and talked about school until Brent needed to take TyAnn home. Robert took some time to say goodbye to his friends, then walked home. He arrived as Brent was still talking to TyAnn on the front porch. Robert didn't want to embarrass either of them, so he waited by the front sidewalk. Brent kissed TyAnn on the cheek, then left. TyAnn waited on the porch for Robert.

"Don't say a word about Brent, okay."

"I wasn't going to, Tanny."

"He is really nice, but I doubt I'll ever go out with him again. He's not my type."

"Oh, you have a 'type' now, huh?"

"Stop it! Come on in. We made ice cream yesterday and there's enough left for a couple bowls."

"You look very nice tonight, TyAnn. Is that a new dress?"

"Thank you, Robert. Yes, it's a new dress. I got it on sale at Steiner's."

"Did Brent tell you how pretty you look?"

"No, he was kinda shy about that stuff."

"Too bad. Maybe if he had complimented you about your dress, he might have gotten a real kiss."

"Oh, no, he wouldn't have. He was lucky I let him kiss my cheek."

Chapter Thirty-Seven

Robert and David both had scholarships to play basketball at SIU. SIU belonged to the "college division" in athletics, which consisted of smaller colleges and universities. Freshman were allowed to participate on the varsity sports teams while they were not at the larger universities. Robert started from the very first game and David was usually the first sub to enter the game. He even started four games. The team finished the season with a record of 20-10. Dad brought TyAnn to several games during the year, and she learned her way around campus. She was seriously considering attending SIU for college. The first game Dad brought TyAnn to was against St. Louis University. They had seats on the bleachers in the upper section of SIU Arena.

"Daddy, why on earth do these colleges have such weird names for their teams? I know what a Saluki is now, but what on earth is a Billekin?"

Dad chuckled shrugged and said, "I'm afraid I don't have a clue. Maybe Robert knows."

"This isn't quite as impressive as the Assembly Hall, but it's all right," she mentioned as she looked around the two-year-old arena.

"It's not as big, but Robert has always dreamed about playing ball here. Not in this building since it just opened in 1964, but I mean for this college."

"Why did he choose Southern? He could have gone to some big time programs. That obnoxious coach from Kansas wanted him. So did Kentucky and Illinois."

"I think he chose Carbondale because it's smaller. He doesn't like the atmosphere at some of the bigger universities. I imagine he will always prefer to live in a small town as opposed to a large city."

"You mean he would rather live in Kinmundy Junction than say... Mount Trenton?"

Dad laughed then said, "I guess I meant a large city like Chicago or St. Louis."

"I know you did. I used to think Mount Trenton was so big, but I know better now."

Even though David was in school on a basketball scholarship, he wanted to try out for the baseball team. Coach Jones told David he could play baseball as soon as basketball season was over. He made the team as a pitcher. He soon became the best starting pitcher on the team. David realized that if he wanted to play sports at the professional level it would be in baseball. He lacked the quickness to play basketball on a higher level. He decided to keep playing both sports as long as he could.

Despite Robert always teasing TyAnn about not going to class, he was a very serious student. He never missed a class, unless the basketball team was gone, and he worked diligently to keep up with his classwork. He sometimes wondered how David managed to handle playing two sports and his heavy class load. Before it seemed possible, their first year at SIU was over.

That summer, after spending a couple weeks going back and forth between home and the farm, Robert asked Mom and Dad, "Would you mind if I stay out at Grandma's during the week and come home on the weekends?"

"Are you sure you want to do that?"

"I could help with the chores a lot easier if I was there all week."

TyAnn offered, "I could come out a couple days to help Grandma in the house and with her flowers."

Mom and Dad agreed to this arrangement. Grandma was grateful to have the kids stay with her. At first, she was reluctant to put them to work.

Robert assured her, "Grandma, we are here to work. You don't need to take care of us. We will be all right. You give us a list of chores, and we will take care of them for you. TyAnn is not afraid to work, and I'll make sure she does a good job."

"Hey, who's going to make sure you get your chores finished?" TyAnn as she poked Robert in the side.

"Don't you two be fighting. I know you will both do a good job. What kind of pie would you like for dessert tonight?"

"Apple, please," Robert requested.

"Blueberry, please, Grandma. I love blueberry pie."

"I guess I will have to make two pies."

"I'll help you..."

"I want Grandma to make the apple pie. You can make your own pie, Tanny."

"What's the matter? Don't you trust me?" TyAnn asked as she grinned.

Grandma soon got used to Robert and TyAnn doing all the chores. They spent most of the summer on the farm. One afternoon, as TyAnn sat on the front porch, she mentioned, "If I ever get married I think I would like to live on a farm like this."

Chapter Thirty-Eight

When school started for her junior year, TyAnn signed up for the school paper, the yearbook staff, Future Housewives of America, auditioned for the fall play and managed to maintain her perfect GPA. She still helped Grandma on the farm in addition to her many school activities. She never seemed to get tired though.

Dad told her, "TyAnn, you should take some time to relax and be lazy like teenagers are supposed to be."

"I can't, Daddy. There are too many things I need to get done."

Dad noticed, though, that sometimes TyAnn would get so sleepy that she would fall asleep while reading her textbooks.

"TyAnn, you need to wake up, honey, so you can go to sleep," Dad would tell her, then laugh.

She would look at him and say, "That makes no sense at all, Daddy."

The junior class was responsible for the yearly Carnival. TyAnn was on all the committees and worked many hours behind the scenes to make Carnival a success. On the night of the Carnival, TyAnn was surprised when she was elected Carnival Queen. In November she was the junior class representative for the homecoming court. Robert and David managed to get home for homecoming. They came to the game alone and both of them danced with TyAnn later. Robert noticed a difference in TyAnn. Gone were most of her tomboy ways. She had grown into a very pretty young lady. Well, she hadn't really grown anymore. She was still the same height as before, and, of course, she hadn't lost all her tomboy ways, as Robert discovered when she played him a game of one-on-one basketball the next afternoon.

"You're still pretty good at basketball, Ty."

"Why, thank you, Robert," she replied as Robert stole the ball from her.

"Hey! That's not fair. I stopped playing for a minute."

"Never stop playing until you hear the whistle. You should know that by now!"

TyAnn still loved to tease her brother; especially about girls.

"Are you ever going to find a girl to go on a date with you?

Oh, silly me! All the girls you know are in college. They are smart enough to know better than go on a date with you."

"Just so you know, I actually went on three dates this year."

"Three dates! What a Romeo you are. Was it three different girls, or did you manage to get a second date with any of them?"

"It was three different girls. I didn't ask any of them for a second date, but I could have. I suppose you are going on dates every week."

"As a matter of fact, my social life has been extremely busy. Last week I went on a date with John Harris, and he's in his last year at Kaskaskia College."

"You better be careful going out with someone that much older than you, Tanny."

"He behaved like a gentleman and didn't even try to kiss me."

"Just be careful, Ty. Some guys behave like lambs on the first date and turn into wolves on the second one."

"I know what some guys are after. I'm not totally ignorant about that."

In the spring TyAnn had to make a decision. On the same day both Brent Gentry and Gary Vandermehr asked her to go to the senior prom.

"Mom, you won't believe what happened today," TyAnn said as she dropped her books on the kitchen table.

"What was it?" Mom asked as she peeled potatoes for supper. "You know where your books belong, and it isn't on the kitchen table."

"Two boys asked me to the prom. Can you believe it?"

"Which two boys, Ty? I bet I know who one of them was," Mom said with a grin. "I bet Brent asked you to go. I talked to his mother at the store a couple days ago, and she said he would probably ask you."

"Brent did ask, but Gary Vandermehr asked me first."

"Did you give the boys an answer?"

"I told them I would decide overnight and tell them in the morning."

"Have you made up your mind?"

"I've been thinking about going with Gary. I did go to

homecoming with Brent. He was a terrible dancer then, and I doubt if he's improved."

"So you're going to go with Gary to protect your feet, huh?" Mom teased.

TyAnn told the boys of her decision the next morning. Brent seemed disappointed, but went right over to Maggie Soldner and asked her. She accepted, so Brent had a date.

On prom night Gary picked TyAnn up. Mom and Dad took enough photos to fill a scrapbook. Gary's talent on the dance floor far surpassed Brent's. TyAnn's feet survived the night without bruises. At ten o'clock, Louise Koskie was crowned as the prom queen. TyAnn and Gary even stayed for the Post Prom, which lasted from one to four in the morning. The parents of the juniors served breakfast and by 4:08, TyAnn was back home. Gary accompanied her to the front porch. TyAnn stood on the first step and faced him. All night long Gary had hoped for a kiss, but she denied him. This was his last chance.

"I had a great time tonight, Ty. I really enjoyed dancing with you."

"It was fun. Please don't tell Brent, but you are a much better dancer."

Gary laughed and said, "An elephant would make a better dance partner." He moved closer and asked, "Can I kiss you, Ty?" He should have kissed her without asking for permission.

"I had a lot of fun, Gary, but I don't want to kiss you."

"How about a kiss on the cheek?"

"No, let's just say good night. I'm really wiped out."

"Okay, good night, Ty. I'll see you in class on Monday."

Chapter Thirty-Nine

During Robert's and David's sophomore year, the Salukis had an even better team. Clyde Walters returned to the team after having to sit out a year because of academic difficulties. Robert and Clyde started as guards, and David was a starting forward. Clarence Smithson, the team's best defender, started at the other forward position. Tall, skinny Ralph Johansson finally earned the starting center position. Coach Don Jones had stuck with Ralph since he was a clumsy freshman who couldn't run down the court without tripping over his own feet. Ralph, now a senior, had shown tremendous improvement, but still exhibited his awkwardness at times. One time he tripped over a loose shoelace, fell and landed in the lap of a cheerleader. A few days later, he hit his head on a low doorway while talking to that same cheerleader. Despite their awkward introduction, two years later they married.

The Salukis had a fantastic year with big upset wins over Louisville and Texas Western. They finished first in the Missouri Valley Conference, but weren't allowed to play in the NCAA tournament because of their status as a member of the college division. Instead they settled for a bid to the National Invitation Tournament. They advanced all the way to the championship game. Their opponent would be the scrappy Marquette Warriors from Milwaukee. Al McGuire, a native of New York City, coached the Warriors. The team took on the same fiery personality as their coach.

Madison Square Garden served as the site for the championship game, and the Salukis were impressed by the arena and their visit to "The Big Apple." They had time for some sightseeing early in the week before the big game. Clyde Walters had grown up in the Bronx, so he acted as tour guide for the team. Robert was impressed with Central Park. The whole team took a trip to the Statue of Liberty and the Empire State Building.

Mom, Dad and TyAnn drove to New York City for the game. They stayed at the Garden Hotel, only five blocks away from Madison Square Garden. Robert managed to spend some time with them on the night before the game.

"Have you seen the important sites?" TyAnn asked.

Robert told her all the places he had seen.

"I liked seeing all the theaters along Broadway. What was your favorite?"

"Well, we didn't get to go inside, but I did see the outside of Yankee Stadium. That was cool."

"I should have known you would like a sports stadium best of all. Do you think you could ever live in a place like this?"

"No way! I'm glad I got a chance to see it, but I wouldn't live in New York City if they gave me the whole dang town." He replied as they listened to the sound of police sirens racing by on the street outside.

The game was a close-fought battle and the lead changed hands over twenty times. With twenty seconds left, and the Salukis trailing by one point, Clyde Walters made a steal and the Salukis headed down court. They called a timeout with only five seconds remaining.

Coach Jones gathered the team around him. He instructed them in the huddle, "They will be double-teaming Clyde, trying to keep the ball out of his hands. Robert, you take the ball out..."

Coach continued to diagram the play for them. They broke the huddle, and Robert had to inbound the ball from the sideline. Robert slapped the ball to start the play. Clyde made a break to the top of the key and was double-teamed as expected. Ralph took his position on the baseline. He set a screen for Clarence. Clarence used Ralph's screen to break open on the far side of the court. David broke toward Robert as his defender left him to double-team Clyde. Robert passed the ball to David and broke for the corner. The defender guarding Robert had turned his head, so he was a step behind. David returned the ball to Robert, and before the buzzer sounded, Robert got off a jumper with perfect shooting form. The ball swished through the net, and the Salukis were champs! Mom, Dad and TyAnn were in the stands cheering as Robert realized his boyhood dream of a last second shot to win the championship.

Chapter Forty

TyAnn began her senior year of high school with an announcement to the family. "I am going to SIU next year to study drama, with the intention of becoming a teacher in that department at SIU after graduation."

Robert looked at her, "Are you sure you want to do that? Maybe you should just get married to Tommy Henderson, since I saw you kissing him on the front porch last night."

"I did not!" TyAnn protested with a look of innocence. "Daddy, don't believe a word he says."

"Oh, I'm sorry, that must had been another girl who looked exactly like you, and was wearing your favorite dress, and just happened to walk into our house right afterward."

TyAnn blushed and turned beet red.

"It was just one kiss and not a very good one at that," TyAnn admitted.

Robert looked at her and smiled. TyAnn looked at him with daggers in her eyes before she smiled shyly and said, "Tommy kissed me before I was ready, so it didn't count."

Dad looked at her as if she was still ten years old. "What were you doing out with Tommy Henderson, and why did he try to kiss you?"

Mom explained to Dad, "She is not a child anymore, dear, and it's about time she went on another date."

"Another date!" Dad exclaimed. "You mean she has gone out on a date before this?" Dad asked excitedly.

"Yes, Daddy! I went to a movie with Brent Gentry last year, and if you remember we even went to homecoming together. John Harris took me out once, and there were a couple other boys too."

Dad looked at Mom and sighed.

"Do you remember when I went to prom last year with Gary Vandermehr?" TyAnn asked Dad.

"Yeah, I guess I do. But I also remember that Gary tried to kiss you, and you wouldn't let him."

Robert just watched and listened.

"Bubby, aren't you going to say anything?" TyAnn queried, expecting more teasing.

"I'm content to just listen, Tanny," Robert replied with a grin.

"High school boys are such juveniles and so gross!" TyAnn muttered as she left the table.

TyAnn had the lead role in the senior play "Trouble Comes A-Calling" written by Max McGee. She had been in a play every year and decided after her first one that she would study drama in school. She kept busy with school activities again this year. Dad was so pleased they lived close to the school because TyAnn seemed to be there more than she was at home. In November TyAnn was voted Homecoming Queen, and Robert was there to see her.

"TyAnn, you are the prettiest homecoming queen this school has ever had," Robert said as he smiled at her.

"Do you really think so?"

"No! Mom told me to tell you that."

"You're such a dork, Robert."

"I'm teasing you. Mom didn't had to tell me to say that. It's what I really think."

TyAnn looked at him wondering if he was still teasing her.

Chapter Forty-One

As a junior Robert continued his streak of starting every game for the Salukis basketball team, and had another great season as he led the team in scoring. David started every game and was the second leading scorer on the team. Although the overall record wasn't as good as last year, they still finished second in the conference. Dad and TyAnn came to as many home games as they could. Mom even came to a couple of games. One weekend in late January, TyAnn came to visit and watch a game by herself. Robert and David were sharing an apartment owned by the university.

"Not a bad place you've got here. I was expecting there to be dirty clothes all over the place, but you guys are kinda neat," TyAnn said.

"Just don't look in the closet in his room," David told TyAnn.

TyAnn looked in Robert's bedroom and was surprised by how neat and orderly it appeared. She started to open the closet door, but Robert stopped her.

"It's a mess in there. I admit it."

Later that night, TyAnn offered to sleep on the couch, and to her dismay Robert agreed.

"Aren't you going to even offer your room to me? You're going to make me sleep on the couch!"

"I'm too tall to sleep on the couch."

"Fine! I'll sleep on the couch, creep."

Robert took TyAnn out to lunch the next day.

"This place seems okay. Is the food any good? I know it's probably cheap because you wouldn't eat here otherwise." TyAnn kept talking and looking around as Robert led her to a table.

"This is our table, Ty," Robert said as he walked up to a girl sitting at a table.

"There's already someone sitting here, Bubby..."

TyAnn's face showed surprise when he leaned down and kissed the girl right on the mouth. He turned to look at TyAnn, who had her mouth and eyes wide open in a look of amazement and incredulity.

"TyAnn, I would like you to meet Miss Kerry Kennedy,"

Robert announced in a very proper voice.

"Kerry, this is my sister, TyAnn Allyson Benjamin."

"I'm very glad to finally meet you, TyAnn. Robert has told me all about you, and I feel like I know you already."

TyAnn looked at Kerry, then at Robert. "I guess you have been keeping a secret from me, Bubby."

Robert smiled as he held the chair for TyAnn to sit down. TyAnn and Kerry hit it off immediately, and were soon talking as if they had been best friends for life. Robert sat quietly and listened as he smiled. After lunch Kerry joined them at the apartment.

TyAnn asked, "Kerry, I don't mean to pry, but have you been helping Robert clean the apartment?"

"I did yesterday because he asked for help."

TyAnn turned to Robert and said, "I should have known you had someone helping clean this place. It was too neat for two slobs like you and David!"

Kerry laughed and said, "You should had seen the place yesterday, TyAnn."

Robert told TyAnn, "I wanted to make a good impression for your first time at the apartment, Tanny."

"You know I love you even if you are a sloppy housekeeper."

"Would you like to go out for pizza, then maybe some dancing, TyAnn?" Kerry asked.

"Sure! That would be fun," TyAnn answered with a smile. "Oh, you probably want to take Robert and David with us, huh?"

"It would be fun just the two of us, but the guys would miss us too much."

Robert was listening and teased the girls back. "You two can go out and have fun. David and I are going to pick up some girls and have a party of our own."

"Good! See, Kerry, we don't have to worry about the guys. They have dreams... I mean plans of their own. We can go out dancing, and find a couple of handsome young men to dance the night away with us."

"Hey! Wait a minute!" Robert hollered.

Kerry walked up to Robert and kissed him. "Do you really think we would go out without you? Get ready and let's go. TyAnn and I are hungry."

146

They had pizza at the nearby Pizza Palace.

"How did you meet Robert?" TyAnn asked while stuffing her face with pizza.

"We had an English Lit class together last semester and started dating soon after," Kerry replied.

TyAnn looked at Robert and announced in a very proper and polite manner, "You're going to get it for keeping Kerry a secret from me, Bubby. I am gonna tickle you to death, or something or other. Do Mom or Dad know yet?"

"Not yet," Robert answered.

"You are an absolute stinker! I have told you about every single date I have ever had. How could you keep quiet about Kerry?" She punched him hard enough in his ribs for him to wince.

"Robert has told me about your nicknames for each other," Kerry said. "I think that's so perfect because I used to call my brother by a special name when we were little."

"Where is your brother now?" TyAnn asked.

Robert kicked her under the table.

"Ow! What was that for?"

"It's okay, Robert," Kerry told him softly and then turned back to TyAnn. "My brother passed away when I was ten years old from Leukemia."

"Oh, Kerry, I'm so sorry. I'm sorry I asked," TyAnn said.

"It's okay. You had no way of knowing."

Later, as they were returning from a trip to the ladies' room, TyAnn gave Kerry a hug and whispered in her ear. "I don't know what I would do if I ever lost Bubby."

After they finished the pizza, the group headed to a ballroom where a local "big band" was playing. They specialized in music from the '30s and '40s. TyAnn watched as Robert and Kerry danced together.

"Would you like to dance, TyAnn?" David asked.

"Sure, look at those two. I never knew Robert could dance like that."

When they were all back at their table TyAnn asked, "Kerry, where did you learn to dance so well?"

"My mother started taking me to dance classes when I was in kindergarten. I love to dance. Now I teach a dance class at school for some of the drama students. Robert has become quite a dancer, too."

"I noticed that. Will you dance with me, Bubby?"

"If Kerry will let me, I will."

"Go ahead. You can dance with Tanny if you want. I will dance with David."

TyAnn and Kerry became best friends, and TyAnn even allowed Kerry to call her Tanny. When Robert heard this, he knew he had found a special girl because she had TyAnn's seal of approval already.

Chapter Forty-Two

TyAnn graduated from high school as the class valedictorian. She had been elected the prom queen, as well. Robert attended her graduation ceremony and listened, with pride, as TyAnn gave her speech. He remembered how she used to walk to school holding his hand because she was frightened. Now she seemed so grown up and self-assured. TyAnn received a scholarship to attend SIU and couldn't wait to join her brother.

One week after TyAnn's graduation, Robert stepped outside calling for Charger, but she didn't come.

"Charger, where are you girl? I have a special treat for you!"

Robert ambled over to the old shed. As he rounded the corner he saw Charger next to the shed. He dropped the treat he was holding in his hand.

"Oh, no," he cried softly.

Robert went in the house to tell TyAnn. Charger was fourteen years old. She had never been sick a day, or in obvious pain to anybody. Robert held TyAnn close to his side, as he almost carried her to see Charger. TyAnn knelt beside her beloved Charger, who had been her lifelong companion, and let the tears flow. Robert knelt beside her and comforted her with his hand on her back.

"We'll have to let Mom and Dad know, Tanny," Bubby whispered.

"Will you tell them? I don't think I can."

Mom and Dad returned home soon after finishing the grocery shopping at the Millstown IGA. TyAnn was in her room on her bed. Robert told Mom and Dad the bad news, and Mom went to see TyAnn. TyAnn held tightly to Mom as they both cried softly. Robert and Dad prepared a place to bury Charger. They chose a spot next to the tree by the old sandbox where Robert and TyAnn played as kids. Robert and Dad built a wooden box for Charger. TyAnn placed the old blanket, that Charger would sleep on, in the box. When the site was ready, the whole family came out to say their final farewell to the fifth member of the family.

"I guess she knew I was going away in the fall, and decided

149

to give me a couple months to get used to the idea of her being gone," TyAnn said.

"We will all miss her, sweetheart, but you were always her favorite. She was your puppy from the start," Mom said as she hugged TyAnn.

TyAnn kept her favorite picture of her and Charger on her nightstand for many years, until she replaced it with a picture of her first child, Isabella.

Chapter Forty-Three

In September of 1968, Robert and TyAnn were both at SIU. Mom and Dad had the house to themselves for the first time in over twenty years. Dad pretended not to be sentimental, but Mom often found him in TyAnn's room looking at her pictures.

"Our baby is all grown up," Dad told Mom one day.

"It happens that way, Jim."

"It seems like only yesterday, she was a little girl in a ponytail. She would sit on my lap, and I would read her a story. Remember how she used to be afraid of storms."

"I remember, Jim. Just because she is growing up, doesn't mean she isn't your little girl anymore."

Dad laughed and said, "Yeah, I haven't had to read a book to her before she goes to bed for a long time."

TyAnn adjusted to campus life quickly because she had her two best friends with her—Robert and Kerry. Robert's final year of basketball was a mixed affair of joy and regret. He was joyful at becoming the school's all time leading scorer, but sad because in the tenth game of the year David suffered a knee injury and would miss the rest of the season. As it turned out, he missed the baseball season, too.

On December 6, 1968, Robert took Kerry out to dinner. They came back to the apartment supposedly to study. Kerry sat on the couch with her feet under her and her English Lit textbook in her hand. She was deep in thought when she felt Robert bump her knee. She looked up and he was on his knee with a small box in his hand.

"Kerry Kennedy, will you marry me?"

She dropped the book. It landed on his foot and he winced in pain. The book weighed over ten pounds.

"Yes! I would marry you tomorrow if we could."

"I don't think I could walk down the aisle tomorrow. My big toe feels like it's broke."

"Silly, you don't have to walk down the aisle. I do."

Robert grinned and said, "I do too. Does that mean we're married?"

Kerry wrapped her arms around him and squeezed. Then

she gave him a long kiss.

Later, Robert told TyAnn and she cried with joy for him. "I'm so happy for you, Bubby!"

"I'm glad you and Kerry are good friends. That means a lot to me."

"It seems like we've known each other for a long time," TyAnn said as she hugged him tightly.

Robert and Kerry planned a June wedding, and Kerry asked TyAnn to be her maid of honor. Robert asked David to be his best man.

The school year passed quickly for TyAnn, but for Robert and Kerry, it seemed to take forever. Robert found a small two-bedroom apartment in Carbondale, close to the campus. TyAnn stayed with Robert for a week after classes were over. It was her last chance to be with her brother before he got married. They visited a bunch of state parks, and other recreational sites, they thought might be interesting. At the Garden of the Gods, TyAnn climbed all over the rock outcrops. She was as nimble as a mountain goat. Robert watched his sister and for a moment remembered her as a child. In his thoughts he heard her say, "Look, Bubby, I can climb so high, and I'm not afraid."

Robert Lee Benjamin and Kerry Lynn Kennedy were married on June 14 in Kerry's hometown of Thorpe, Illinois, in Surrey county. The small, wood-frame Baptist church was packed with family and friends. Kerry's father proudly walked her down the aisle. Robert's heart fluttered as he saw his future bride in her wedding gown for the first time.

"Wow!" David said as he leaned closer to Robert.

Robert smiled and said, "Double wow! Did you ever think a girl that gorgeous would fall for a guy like me?"

David shook his head and whispered, "Never in a million years. You've got funny looking ears."

The preacher was listening and looked at Robert. He put a hand to his mouth to stifle a laugh.

Finally, Kerry stood next to him and Robert smiled. TyAnn tried not to look at Robert because she knew she would start to cry. It didn't work! She cried anyway.

After the honeymoon, Kerry moved into the apartment with Robert. She quickly transformed the apartment into their home by adding some feminine touches. Plus, she made Robert put his basketball trophies away. After attending a couple of summer basketball camps, and discussing his options with his father and Coach Jones, Robert decided to pass up a shot at pro basketball to work on his master's degree. Kerry had one more year of school to finish. Robert accepted a job working as an assistant to Coach Jones on the SIU basketball team. He also taught physical education classes to make enough money to support himself and Kerry.

David Tomanek received his bachelor's degree and immediately started working on his masters. He later earned a doctorate in education. He accepted a position at the school, and over the years, worked his way up to become the Dean of Men and later president of the university.

TyAnn worked very diligently toward a double major and finished school in three and a half years. After she graduated, TyAnn realized her dream by getting a job in the school's drama department.

When Coach Jones retired, Robert Benjamin became the head varsity basketball coach of the SIU Salukis.

Chapter Forty-Four

During her years at SIU, TyAnn would spend the summers helping Grandma on the farm. The uncles, and their sons, took care of most of the major work on the farm, and kept the place in as good of condition as if Grandpa was still alive. It took a lot of hard work and sacrifice, but they did it for Grandma.

"Grandma, will you tell me how you met Grandpa?" TyAnn asked her one day.

"Oh, child, that was so long ago. I'm not sure I remember exactly, but I'll tell you what I can remember."

Grandma and TyAnn sat on the front porch swing as Grandma began. "I was born in Bohemia when it was still a country, long time ago. When I was twelve years old, my brothers and I came to this country. We settled in Chicago where some of our other relatives and friends from Bohemia lived. I went to school for a while but then had to quit to get a job and help support the family. My brothers operated a little grocery store on the corner, and we lived upstairs in the apartment above it. One day a few years later, a very handsome man came in to buy some groceries. He started talking to my brother in Bohemian. That was your grandfather, child. I was working in the store, but was too shy to talk to him. He looked at me and smiled. He started coming in to the store almost every day or so to buy meat and other groceries. Finally, I got up enough nerve to talk to him when he asked me my name. I told him my name and he told me his and where he was from. We were both from Bohemia and lived in towns not far apart. He came to this country several years before I did and lived in Cleveland for a time before he moved to Chicago with his brother John. He told me he had a job working at the Western Electric plant in Cicero, and he took the bus to work everyday. After a few weeks he asked me to go to the dance at the local dancehall. We dated for several months, then he asked me to marry him."

"Oh, Grandma, that is so romantic!" TyAnn told her in a dreamy voice, as she hugged Grandma.

"We got married and lived in a small apartment close to the store and my family. I told you what happened shortly after we were married, didn't I?"

"You mean the Eastland," TyAnn answered.

"Oh, that was a terrible day!" Grandma shuddered as she told TyAnn. "Anyway, your Uncle Gus was born in Chicago, and shortly after that Grandpa told me we were moving to southern Illinois to live on a farm. I cried because I didn't want to leave my family. Well, to make a long story shorter, we moved here, and Grandpa built this farm. I haven't been back to Chicago in so many years."

"Do you still miss your family, Grandma? You still have a sister up north, right?" TyAnn asked.

"I miss them, but so many years have passed," Grandma replied with a faraway look on her face. Grandma would never think of anywhere else but the farm as her home.

One day, in the early part of her senior year at SIU, TyAnn was studying in the library when a handsome young man sat down at her table to read. They exchanged glances at each other for about a half hour. TyAnn smiled at him with the hope he would talk to her. She finished her studies, but didn't leave. She kept reading her book and sneaking glances at the young man. Finally, just before she was going to leave, he had the courage to talk to her.

"Hello, my name is Michael Conor O'Shay, and I'm originally from Ireland."

"Hi, I'm TyAnn Benjamin, and I'm from Kinmundy Junction. I could tell by your accent that you weren't from around here," TyAnn said as she giggled like a young schoolgirl.

"My family lives in South Baden now. That's not too far from Kinmundy Junction."

"Yes, I've been there a few times."

They talked for a few minutes, then Michael asked, "Would you like to go somewhere and get something to drink? We are supposed to be quiet in the library, and I would really like to talk with you."

"I am rather thirsty. There is an old-fashioned soda shop a few blocks away."

"I think I know the place. I've passed it by, but have never gone inside. We don't have anything like that back home in Ireland."

The afternoon was sunny and warm, so Michael and TyAnn walked over to the soda shop. They were there until dark. They forgot to eat supper because they were so interested in each other. Michael asked TyAnn to dinner the next night, and she agreed. After dating for a couple weeks, TyAnn brought Michael over to meet Robert and Kerry. They had dinner together and after Michael left, TyAnn talked to Robert.

"Well, what do you think?"

"I think we are going to have a good team this year."

TyAnn and Kerry both smacked Robert on his arms.

"Oh, you want to know about Michael, I suppose."

"Yes, do you like him?"

Robert looked at TyAnn, and he knew she was in love. "I like him very much. He seems like a good guy, and I can tell that he loves you as much as you obviously love him."

"What do you think, Kerry?"

"I agree with Robert, though not about the basketball team."

They all laughed.

"Seriously, I think he's a keeper, Tanny."

A month later TyAnn brought Michael home to meet her parents. Michael was a bit nervous because Robert had told him that their father was very protective of TyAnn and had never liked any of her other boyfriends.

"Don't believe Robert. Daddy is very nice, but sometimes he thinks I am still his little girl. And by the way, I have dated a number of guys, but I never considered any of them to have been "boyfriends" like you."

"That's a relief. I feel better about meeting your parents now."

TyAnn and Michael fell head-over-heals in love. One night Michael and TyAnn were walking arm in arm through the freshly fallen snow after having dinner together. The air was cool and crisp and the stars were twinkling in the night sky as they talked. They stopped for a moment and Michael kissed her. Then he got on his knee and asked, "TyAnn Benjamin, will you do me the honor of becoming my wife?"

She got on her knees and wrapped her arms around his neck. "Yes! Yes! Yes! I will marry you, Michael O'Shay!"

They were both on their knees as they hugged and kissed. When they stood up after a couple minutes, they noticed several other students were watching them.

"We're getting married!" Micheal proudly proclaimed.

The students applauded.

TyAnn told Michael, "I want to go tell Robert and Kerry, if that's okay with you."

Robert and Kerry lived a couple blocks away, so it didn't take long for TyAnn and Michael to run over to their apartment. Robert opened the door to let them in.

"Hey, guys. What are you two up to tonight?" Robert asked as Kerry walked into the room. Kerry took one look at TyAnn and knew somehow had happened.

"We're getting married! Michael just proposed to me and I accepted!" TyAnn exclaimed as her face shone with happiness. "I said yes!"

"Oh, Tanny, I'm so happy for you," Kerry said as they hugged each other.

"Congratulations, Michael," Robert told him as he shook his hand. Robert then turned to TyAnn and gave her a hug as he lifted her off her feet and twirled her around.

"Are you happy for me, Bubby?" TyAnn asked as she noticed tears in her brother's eyes.

"I'm very happy for you, Tanny." For a split second he thought of teasing her, but he didn't. "I'm so very happy for you!"

Michael took TyAnn home to meet his parents, and they also fell in love with her immediately. Michael and TyAnn decided to get married at the farm so Grandma could be at the wedding of her only granddaughter. The date was set for June 10.

It was a very simple wedding with only family and close friends in attendance. They set up a large tent in the yard to use in case of rain. As it turned out, they didn't need it for the ceremony. The sun shone brightly with fluffy white clouds in the sky. They did use the tent later for the reception. Some of the cousins set up the rented chairs on the east side of the house. TyAnn had always thought it was the prettiest part of the yard because of all the flowers Grandma had planted there. The chairs were facing the rose garden where Michael, Robert and the preacher would stand. Kerry was TyAnn's matron of honor and Robert was Michael's best man. Dad walked her down the aisle as one of their friends from college played an Irish love song on his acoustic guitar. Michael's parents were there and everyone had a hard time understanding their Irish accent. Of course, his parents had just as hard a time understanding her family as well. When it came time to say her vows, TyAnn's voice was heard loud and clear. Robert watched Tanny with tears in his eyes as he remembered the little girl who had been his best friend all these years. The preacher pronounced them husband and wife, and Michael kissed his new bride. The reception was held immediately afterward.

TyAnn had wanted something unusual and she got her wish. The family had an old-fashioned gathering like when she and Robert were kids. Grandma and all the ladies cooked enough food to feed the SIU football team. TyAnn even stood on the ice cream maker to help steady the bucket which allowed Dad, then Robert, to finish making the homemade ice cream. Michael had never had this treat before, and Robert challenged him to an ice cream eating contest. Michael and Robert both got "brain-freezes."

TyAnn shook her head as she told them, "You should know better than to eat so fast, Bubby, and shame on you for making Michael do the same thing. Now off with the both of you," TyAnn replied with an Irish accent that made both guys look at her with funny smiles on their faces.

"What? I am a drama major. Don't you think I can do an Irish accent if I want?"

Later, Grandma was sitting in her rocker on the front porch as she enjoyed having her family together for such a grand occasion. Everybody was there, except for Grandpa, and TyAnn could feel him there in spirit. Before it got too dark, TyAnn took Michael on a tour of the farm. She showed him the orchards and told him about the snake in the machine shed. She took Michael to the pond to show him where they used to fish as kids. She told Michael with an impish look on her face, "I used to go swimming here with Bubby when we were younger."

"Maybe we can continue that tradition soon. We Irish are

big on traditions," Michael told TyAnn as he kissed her as the sun set gloriously behind them.

Michael and TyAnn stayed at the farm until ten o'clock. They changed clothes and were ready to start on their way. TyAnn had not told anyone except Mom where they were spending their first night. Not even Robert was able wheedle the information out of her. Before they left, she saw Dad and hugged him as he cried. TyAnn kissed Mom good night as they hugged tightly. The last person she saw before leaving was Robert. Robert and Michael shook hands and Robert gave him a hug. Robert turned to TyAnn and she opened her arms for him to hold her. They shared a quiet moment together and whispered in each other's ears words that no one else could hear. Robert kissed her on her cheek as she cried.

"Oh, Bubby," she said as he squeezed her tight.

"Take care of Tanny," Robert told Michael.

"You know I will. I love her very much."

Michael opened the door for TyAnn and she got in the car. She waved goodbye to everyone as they drove away. Kerry joined Robert as he stood and watched for a moment after the car had disappeared down the hill.

"I think there is a little bit of ice cream left," Kerry said.

He smiled at her and kissed her tenderly. "I might just have room for one more bowl."

Chapter Forty-Five

Grandma Anna Tomanek lived long enough to see three more great grandchildren born. Robert and Kerry had a son they named Kevin in honor of Kevin Ambuehl, who had drowned shortly after his first year of college. David and his wife Shari had a daughter named Merilyn. TyAnn and Michael had a beautiful daughter they named Isabella Jane.

Mom and Dad Benjamin were the only ones who could afford to buy Grandma and Grandpa's farm after Grandma passed away. They wanted to keep it in the family, and did so. TyAnn and Michael spent their summers staying at the farm for several years. Michael loved to go swimming with his young wife, and they spent many hours strolling about the farm, arm in arm. A couple of years later TyAnn and Michael had twin sons. They were named Benjamin Michael and James Robert. A few days later, Robert and Kerry had a daughter they named Emma Anne after her grandmother. After Grandma Tomanek's death, a total of twelve more babies were born into the family. David and Shari had a total of seven kids and purchased a large farm outside of Carbondale. Robert and Kerry bought the adjacent farm a couple of years later. TyAnn and Michael purchased an older two-story home in Carbondale. Michael started a small business in Carbondale selling and fixing computers. The business thrived in the college town. Michael later sold the business and opened an investment office. He and TyAnn had a comfortable, if not exactly wealthy, life together.

James Lee Benjamin died of a stroke three months before he was ready to retire from teaching at the Kinmundy Junction high school. Mom was shocked as were all the family members. Uncle Charlie told his younger sister at the funeral service, "He was always in such good health. He was never sick. I don't think I ever knew him to be sick a day in his life."

Mom continued to teach second grade until she retired a few years later. It grieved her that she had been unable to keep the farm in the best condition after Dad passed away. One night when Robert, TyAnn and David and their spouses were home visiting,

Mom told them, "I need to do something with the farm. I can't keep it in good enough shape and don't have the finances to continue putting money into it. We need to come up with a plan."

"I think we can come up with a way to keep the farm in the family. I know that would be important to Grandma and Grandpa," Robert said.

For several weeks the kids discussed what should be done with the farm. They all agreed that it needed to be kept in the family somehow. They were all working in Carbondale and couldn't spend enough time at the farm themselves. Robert met with the school's attorney, and they came up with a plan. Robert, David and TyAnn formed a partnership and purchased the farm from Mom. They divided the responsibilities of managing the farm among themselves. They were in a position to be able to afford to pay for the work that needed to be done on a weekly basis. They all spent some time at the farm in the summers, and managed to keep the place in good enough shape that Grandma and Grandpa would have been proud.

A few weeks later Robert, David and Michael decided to build a small "hunting" lodge on top of the hill that overlooked the pond. The wives were jealous because the guys told them it was just for the men, and no women would be allowed inside. TyAnn discussed this with Robert one night.

"If we aren't allowed in your 'hunting lodge,' or whatever you want to call it, then maybe we won't let you guys back in our real homes."

"You know we're just kidding, right?"

"I know. How are we going to make sure we all don't want to use the house at the same time?"

"I figure the wives will have to decide that. We guys don't care if we are all there at the same time."

"I think that will be a perfect spot for a little vacation home. I will get Kerry and Shari together so we can decorate the inside. We can plant flowers all around the yard and..."

"Hold on just a second there, Mrs. O'Shay! This is not going to be some 'feminine' hunting lodge. We want it to be rugged and masculine looking."

"Whatever you want, Bubby!"

Robert knew the women would have their way, so he shrugged his shoulders in resignation.

One afternoon on a warm summer day in July, Emma Benjamin was sitting on the front porch of the farm in Grandma's old rocking chair taking a nap. The sun was shining brightly. The blue sky was filled with fluffy white clouds and there was a gentle breeze blowing through the trees. She could smell the flowers as she reminisced about days gone by.

Three-year-old Isabella Jane O'Shay came up to her and tugged on her arm. Emma opened her eyes, smiled, then leaned down. Isabella whispered in her ear, "Grandma, will you tell me what it was like to live on the farm when you were a little girl."

TyAnn listened at the screen door as Isabella sat on Grandma's lap and Grandma began, "When I was just a little girl...

Epilogue

Charlie Tomanek was the last of all the siblings and spouses to pass away. He lived to be ninety-six. Although his last six months had been spent in a nursing home in Millstown, he maintained his sense of humor and love for people until the end. One night he fell asleep and didn't wake up. Peacefully, he rejoined his beloved Mary.

Robert, TyAnn and their families joined with all the other cousins and friends to say goodbye. It seemed sad to them that the only time the whole family reunited anymore was at occasions like this. The family gathered at the small country church, that Uncle Charlie attended his whole life, for the memorial service. Later, a short trip down a dusty gravel farm road brought everyone to Martin Cemetery. The wind blew gently through the large maple trees that surrounded the old hilltop cemetery. The sun shone brightly as the frail old preacher leaned on his cane as he said a few final words. After Charlie was laid to rest, Robert and TyAnn walked over to see the headstone of Grandma and Grandpa Tomanek.

Robert told his sister, "I want to take a drive into town."

"Would you like some company?" TyAnn asked.

"Would you mind going with me?"

"Not at all. I haven't been to town for quite a while. I want to see the old place."

They returned to their families. Robert told Kerry, "TyAnn and I are going to take a quick run into town. We will meet you at the church in a little while."

Kerry instinctively knew that he wanted to have some time alone with TyAnn.

"I'll ride with Kevin and help take care of our new grandson."

"Do you want me to drive you into town, Dad?" Kevin asked.

"You don't need to. TyAnn is going with me. I'll let her drive. You stay with Brandy and Ty Robert. It looks like they need you."

"Do you have your phone with you?"

"I've got it, or else your mother has it. We won't be gone

too long. Start eating without us," Robert instructed Kevin.

"Oh, we will, don't worry about that," Kevin replied with a grin.

Robert looked at his son. Perhaps it was because they were at a cemetery, or maybe because he was simply feeling nostalgic, but he remembered his old friend, Kevin Ambuehl. He was the reason he named his son Kevin. He thought about the day of his funeral and recalled the cemetery outside of LaGrove where he lay. He remembered visiting the gravesite a few years ago and thought he should return soon.

Robert and TyAnn got in his car and drove away from the cemetery and headed toward Kinmundy Junction. First they drove past their grandparents' old farm. They parked the car and got out. They paused for a few minutes as they looked around. Although some of the out-buildings had been gone for years, the house, barn, machine shed and corn crib were still there. The pond survived as well as the fruit orchards. The house had a fresh coat of white paint and a new roof.

"Looks like David has been busy," Robert told TyAnn as he pointed toward the house.

"It helps to have two sons in the construction business. I'm sure Robbie and John did the work."

TyAnn noticed the pretty flowers in the front yard.

"Look at the flowers, Robert. They are just like Grandma would want."

They returned to the car and spent the few minutes it took to drive across the river and into town quietly lost in their own thoughts and memories. They took a side street to the old downtown area. The town had slowly changed over the years. There were some new buildings downtown, but only one grocery store.

Robert told TyAnn, "I bet you can't put your groceries on a ledger anymore."

TyAnn looked at him and asked, "I wonder if they still sell baseball cards?"

They headed to the cemetery to visit Mom and Dad's resting place. Someone had put out fresh flowers.

"Probably Isabella," TyAnn thought out loud, knowing her daughter so well.

They headed back downtown, crossed the Illinois Central tracks and angled to the right. The road led to the high school. They parked in the lot and got out. The old high school building, where they spent so much time, and gym, where Robert starred on the basketball team, had been gone for years. The big new gym, built two years after Robert graduated, even looked old now.

Robert tried to remember. "How long have I been the head coach at SIU?" he asked TyAnn.

"Thirty-four years. Almost as long as I have been teaching in the theater department," TyAnn replied.

Robert gazed at the spot where the old gym used to stand. He closed his eyes and remembered the sound of sneakers on the wooden court, the crowds cheering and could even remember the shrill sound of the scoreboard horn. He chuckled and said, "I remember when you were the Hornets' team manager. You were so young and little."

"I did a good job, though."

"Yes, you did!"

"Let's go by the house," TyAnn whispered.

Robert started to get in the car, but she stopped him.

"Let's walk, lazy bones. It will be good for you."

They slowly walked the short block and a half, and stopped in front of the old house where they grew up.

TyAnn teased Robert, "It didn't use to take you this long to walk from the school to home."

He smiled in spite of the pain in his knees and hips. They ambled up the driveway and opened the gate to the fenced-in backyard.

"The kids need to mow the yard," Robert said as he looked around at the home where he and TyAnn grew up and where Isabella and her husband Boston Boyer and little girl Tanny Lynn now lived. TyAnn saw a young black Labrador puppy playing in the back yard.

"Look, Robert! Boston and Isa have a new puppy. She didn't tell me that."

"Boston mentioned it to me. I don't remember if I was supposed to tell you, or if it was supposed to be a secret."

"Do you know what they named the puppy?"

Robert grinned at TyAnn and said, "Do you really have to

165

ask?"

TyAnn smiled and called out, "Charger! Come here boy!"

The puppy heard his name and came galloping. TyAnn knelt to pet Charger as he wagged his tail a mile a minute. She let Charger lick her face.

"Go back and wait for Isabella and Boston to come home," TyAnn told Charger and he obeyed.

Robert looked around the yard. The old shed with the dirt floor still stood. The kids even had a garden area in the same place as when he and TyAnn lived here.

"Oh, Tanny, I have so many good memories of this place," Robert whispered to TyAnn after they had been standing silently for a brief moment.

"Come on, Bubby. Let's go back to the church and have some lunch with everybody. The kids will eat everything if we don't get there soon," TyAnn told him gently, as she saw the tears in his eyes. TyAnn looked back one last time to a large tree with a sandbox underneath filled with plastic toys. Robert saw where TyAnn was looking.

"Grandma, there is another little girl called Tanny, with her own Charger, living here now."

TyAnn smiled and whispered, "Don't forget you're a grandpa, too."

"I'm not Grandpa. I'm 'Gra,' remember?"

They shared a laugh as they closed the gate to the backyard. TyAnn took Robert's arm and helped keep him steady as they slowly made their way back to the car. Robert paused for a moment as TyAnn opened the door for him. He closed his eyes and, just for a few seconds, he pictured the old high school building as it was in the days he and TyAnn were students. He could feel the wind on his face. He saw the large maple trees with their leaves fluttering. He pictured a young boy standing on the steps waving his arms. He imagined seeing the open windows of the math classroom in the far corner of the second floor. He smiled as he heard a teacher's voice carried by the gentle breeze. "I still miss you, Dad," he whispered.

On the way out of town, just past the ball diamond at the curve in the old state highway, set in front of the old railroad water tower, used to be a sign. The town had placed it there in 1966. TyAnn slowed the car for a moment to see if it still existed. She smiled as she saw that it did. An old gold-colored sign with faded purple letters.

WELCOME TO KINMUNDY JUNCTION
STATE BASKETBALL CHAMPS 1965